Beyond the Badlands

George Tate was a stubborn man, and he'd sworn no owlhoot gang was going to run him off his own range. Just the same, when the tall capable-looking stranger rode in, Tate was glad to sign him on with no questions asked. The name the stranger gave was Green.

Tate looked him over, and decided that he might be a lot of things, that saturnine newcomer with the tied-down forty-fives . . . but green wasn't one of them!

Beyond the Badlands

Frederick H. Christian

A Black Horse Western

ROBERT HALE · LONDON

DORSET COUNTY COUNCIL	
Cypher	13.03.05
	£10.75

© 1966, 2005 Frederick Nolan
First hardcover edition 2005
Originally published in paperback as
Sudden Strikes Back by Frederick H. Christian

ISBN 0 7090 7641 X

Robert Hale Limited
Clerkenwell House
Clerkenwell Green
London EC1R 0HT

The right of Frederick Nolan to be identified as
author of this work has been asserted by him
in accordance with the Copyright, Designs and
Patents Act 1988.

Typeset by
Derek Doyle & Associates, Liverpool.
Printed and bound in Great Britain by
Antony Rowe Limited, Wiltshire

ONE

'Back off, mister, or I'll blow yu to hellangone!'

The voice quavered slightly, but only because the speaker was no longer a young man. No trace of fear showed in his upright bearing. The late sunlight caught his white hair, and picked out wicked highlights on the twin barrels of the shotgun presently threatening the rider facing him. This was a tall, black-haired cowboy dressed in neat, but well-worn range clothes, indistinguishable from the average cowpuncher except for the twin revolvers in crossed belts strapped about his hips.

'Steady, ol' timer,' said the cowboy, raising his hands. His voice came low-pitched but steady, and without anxiety. 'Yu might sneeze an' plumb ruin my health.'

'I might just do that anyways,' snapped the old man.

'Be obliged if yu'd let me water my horse first.'

'Git!' repeated the oldster. 'Crawl back to yore boss Barclay an' tell him next time to come hisself.'

The tall cowboy shrugged. 'OK, seh,' he said, his voice still mild. 'Wouldn't do no good to tell yu I never heard o' anyone called Barclay, I suppose?'

'Nope.' The old man hesitated for a moment. 'Barclay send yu down here to git me while my boys was on the range?'

'Look, mister, I told you once – I don't know any Barclay.'

'Shore. An' I'm the Queen o' Sheba,' rapped out the old man. 'Yu slipped up if yu figgered to catch me alone, gunman. Take a look at the second window to the right o' the door.'

The cowboy's eyes scanned the windows of the ranch house quickly, and his keen gaze immediately caught the gleam of light on a rifle barrel protruding from the designated window.

'My cook,' explained the rancher. 'He's a good cook. He's even better at shootin'. Take two steps the wrong way an' yo're a dead man. Allus supposin' that yo're stupid enough to try it.'

'Yu must figger someone wants yore hide pretty bad.'

'I figger yore skulkin' boss Barclay wouldn't stop at nothin' to get what he wants. Now—' Once again the gesture with the shotgun. 'We're through palaverin'. Roll yore tail.'

The cowboy sighed, his face a study in tried patience.

'Look, I'll try her once more. My name's James Green – yu can see the brand on the hoss here – and I'm from Texas. I stopped here because I figgered yu'd let me use yore water. I never heard o' nobody named Barclay, an' I shore ain't over keen to get to know him on the basis o' what yo're sayin'. But if I'd'a been tryin' to salivate yu I shore wouldn't have ridden up to yore front yard an' knocked afore I tried.'

The old man looked at the black-haired cowboy for a long, long moment, and his gaze slid slowly to the butts of the six-shooters nestling low in their holsters, the dull-shining handles eloquent testimony to much use. The cowboy returned this piercing scrutiny calmly. With a short nod, as if coming to a decision, the old man eased the hammers of his shotgun down, half-turned towards the house, calling 'Cookie, yu put down that shootin' arn an' lay out a cup of java for this young feller. He shore ain't got the cut o' one o' Barclay's bar-scourin's now as I think about it.' Then turning back towards the cowboy, he smiled and thrust out his hand. 'I'm George Tate, owner o' this spread – the Slash 8. Light an' water yore horse, Mr Green.'

'That's the formal handle, seh,' admonished the smiling cowboy as he dismounted. 'Jim comes a sight easier.'

George Tate led the way into the house. Green followed him after loosening his horse's saddle-girth and allowing the stallion a quick drink at the watering trough. He found himself in a spacious living room, dominated by a huge stone fireplace before which lay scattered several mountain lion pelts. The wood floor was bare, but scrubbed to a bone white. The furniture was simple and robust, and the generally cluttered and untidy air spoke of a bachelor establishment. Green, covertly assessing his host, guessed that Tate was a widower of many years standing and the old man, as if guessing the thoughts of the younger, said gruffly, 'Wife's been dead a heap o' years, Jim. Apaches.' The one single grim word and the way it was spoken were enough. Green knew that this man's blood was in the land here. He would die before he'd run.

The short silence was interrupted by the entrance of a small, wrinkled, dark-visaged man of uncertain age, who surveyed the cowboy with eyes snapping with humour. 'Shore glad yu didn't get the twitches while yu was a-sittin' out there,' he grinned, showing evil, brown teeth, 'or I'd just by-cracky nacherly salivated yu. Mind yu,' he continued, 'I'd a been right sorry when I found out yu wasn't one of King's men.'

Green looked a question, and his host explained, 'Everyone calls Zack Barclay, "King", account of he claims he's King o' the valley. That four flusher come to these parts about two years ago. Had nothin' but trouble since.'

'What kind o' trouble?' asked Green.

'Ev'ry damn kind there is, Jim.' Tate put down the coffee cup which his cook had handed him, and lit up a battered old pipe. 'Not that there's anythin' provable. But we've had rustlin', an' killin', an' this Shadders gang....'

'Suppose yu tell Jim the story from the beginnin', boss,' interjected the cook. 'He don't rightly know what yo're talkin' about.'

The old man glared at his cook, who smiled back unperturbed.

'Dang me, Cookie . . . ' his mock anger subsided into another chuckle, 'if yu ain't about right. She was like this, Jim. Barclay come to these parts about two years ago. Bought the old Casey spread. Rebuilt the ranch house, restocked the range, hired a tough crew.'

'Tell him about the rustlin',' interjected Cookie.

'Ain't yu got no chores to be doin'?' growled Tate. 'Where was I . . . oh, yes. About two, three months after Barclay arrove, we – that's me an' the others hereabouts – noticed we was losin' cattle. Nothin' serious. Ten head, twenty. It was unusual, but it didn't bother none of the bigger spreads. Hangin' Rock – that's the nearest town to here – started buzzin' with rumours about some outlaw gang called the Shadders that'd holed up on the southern end o' Thunder Mesa, them mountains over to the south, there.'

'I'm takin' it that it wasn't no rumour, then,' put in Green.

'Yo're durn right it warn't,' flashed the old rancher. 'After a while, it got more obvious. Took on a pattern, sorta. They was only hittin' the smaller ranchers. One by one, them people found they didn't have enough beef to market. No beef, no money. No money, yu can't pay yore debts. Then the Bank has to foreclose. Afore yu could say Jehosophat, Barclay bought up them ranches for a song.'

'Nothin' criminal in that, seh,' opined Green.

'Agreed, agreed,' said the old man testily. 'Wait 'til I'm through. After a while I began to realise that Barclay owned quite a piece o' this valley. Anyways, all the land on the north side o' the Sweetwater – that's the river yu musta crossed on yore way into the valley.'

Green nodded.

'Seen Barclay in town one day,' Tate told him. 'Taxed him with the whole thing. He smiled like one o' them Chessy cats and says to me, "Tate, they ain't no law against buyin' land. I aim to own this whole valley come next Spring, one way or the other." I said that he'd git my ranch over my dead body, an' he looks at me cold as an undertaker. "I shore hope that won't prove necessary," he says.'

'Ain't yu got a sheriff?' the cowboy asked.

'We ain't – but Barclay has,' was the meaningful reply. 'Biggest misfit the Good Lord ever put ears on, an' that's sayin' plenty. Anyways, what could we do? Barclay ain't stepped outside o' the Law, an' all the rest has been pinned on the Shadders.'

'All the rest?'

'Shucks, I'm about to tell yu: no need to rush me. After it became obvious that them who was goin' to quit – for one reason or another – had sold out an' gone, the bigger spreads started gettin' visitors."

'The Shadows?'

'I'm guessin' so, although nobody that's been involved has been what yu'd call chattery about it. Far as I c'n tell, three or four fellers wearin' masks would ride up to a ranch at night, call out the owner, and talk awhile. Tom Sheppard was the first one they talked to. He moved out real quick. Nary a word to anyone.'

'Whereupon friend Barclay bought the ranch off the bank,' mused Green.

'Like yu say,' agreed Tate. 'Next in line was Harry Carpenter. Same thing. Sold the Box 40 for what he could get. Piled his wife an' kids into a wagon, an' pulled his freight.'

'They was told to move on ... or else.'

'Exactly. Then it all come to a head. A couple o' weeks ago, Jess Stackpole over at the Diamond S – that's just over the hill a mile or two from here – got a night visit. Stepped out to talk to them over the barrel of his gun. Fool play. Shot dead in his own yard, he was, right in front o' his woman an' kids. Brady rode out there, clucked around the yard like some fool hen. Couldn't find nothin', o' course. I misdoubt he could find Texas if he was standin' in San Antone.'

'An' yu, seh?'

'Well, like yu saw, Jim, I been expectin' company ever since they hit the Stackpole place. Barclay's bought that, of course. Which leaves me the only ranch left on this side of the valley that Barclay ain't bought.'.

'Which is why yu jumped me out there.'

'Shore, son, I wish yu'd overlook that. If I'd known....'

'Shucks, no need to apologise, seh,' said Green. 'Better to make that kind o' mistake an' be proved wrong than to make Stackpole's kind.'

The old rancher's face turned grim, and a short silence ensued. Knocking out his pipe against the stone fireplace, he rose and went to the window through which he peered into the yard. 'No sign of the boys, yet,' muttered Tate.

'How many men yu got?' Green asked him.

'On'y five,' replied the old man. 'Used to have eight, but the others kinda – drifted. Can't say as I blame them. They probably seen trouble shapin' up an' they didn't want in. Makes things a mite difficult around the place, but we manage.'

Cookie announced, 'I'm makin' apple pie. I figger yu'll stay fer supper, Jim?'

'Shucks, it completely slipped my mind to ask yu, Jim,' said Tate, slapping his leg. 'Course yo're stayin', young feller. Least we could do to make up for the reception yu got!'

Green admitted that he'd admire to sample fresh apple pie. The old man came out on to the porch and pointed out the bunkhouse and the stables.

'Yu go an' unpack yore gear, feed yore hoss. Yo're stayin' over the night, whether yu like it or not.'

Whereupon the old rancher clumped back into the house, leaving the cowboy to lead the black stallion over to the stable.

Green reflected on the activities of Barclay and his outfit as he methodically did the chores of caring for his horse.

'Why would he want all the land in the valley, though, Thunder?' The horse nickered in response to his name. 'He's got plenty of access to the river, an' all the grazin' land he can use....'

His soliloquy was obviously unsatisfactory; anyone watching Green would have seen him stop as though struck by a thought, then shake his head, and then go about his tasks once more.

'Seems ridiculous enough, Thunder,' he told his horse, 'to be probably true. I wonder whether Barclay employs the Shadows ... or they employ him?'

At that moment, he tensed as the sound of several horses came through the open doorway from the yard; but he relaxed as he told himself that it was probably Tate's riders in from the range. He idled over to a window to catch a glimpse of the Slash 8 crew in time to see four riders come to a milling halt before the verandah of the ranch. Soundlessly, Green moved back from the window, the glint of light on drawn guns showed that these men were on no friendly errand.

Outside, the leader of the quartet shouted in a thick, grating voice: 'Tate, come out, yu ol' buzzard!'

A moment or two passed, and then the old man came out of the house, the same shotgun with which he had threatened Green canted menacingly towards the four men facing him on horseback.

'Buzzard, is it?' he snapped. 'An' who sent yu, big mouth?' Before the leader had even time to open his mouth, Tate went on, 'Don't tell me, let me guess. Yore boss Barclay sent yu. Well, yu came. Now turn round an' git. Whatever yu came for, the answer's no.'

The leader dismounted. He was a big man, dressed in the common garb of the range seen everywhere in that country. As he approached Tate, the other three dismounted in unison and fanned out behind their leader so that Tate was forced to keep the shotgun barrel weaving in an arc to cover them. The big man spoke again.

'I got a message for yu from The Shadows – get out of the valley, an' get out fast. The air 'round here is bad for yore health. If yu stay, it might prove – fatal.'

'Well, damn me if yu ain't got more gall than a Pawnee Injun,' crackled old George Tate, his voice tight with anger. 'Yu climb back on yore nag and take this message back to King Barclay. Tell him I'll see him in Hell afore I'll move off my range. An' tell yore friends ahind yu there to keep their itchy feet still, or yu'll be cartin' them home belly down.'

'Yu shore are the tough one, ain't yu?' jeered the leader of the quartet. 'Anyone'd think yu had someone in the house there backin' yore play.'

The import of the big man's leering tone suddenly

registered on Tate, and on the hidden watcher in the barn at the same time. Moving like a prowling cat, Green headed silently through the stables and around out of sight behind the outbuildings. Meanwhile Tate's uncertainty was deepening. 'Yu figgerin' on yore cook backin' yu up, old man? Why don't yu give him a shout?' The big man laughed as at some huge joke, and Tate called, without turning his head, 'Cookie! Cookie, are yu all right?' The silence was deathly. Unwittingly, Tate turned his head to call again, giving the big man an opportunity which he seized instantly. With a tigerish leap, the intruder grabbed the barrel of the shotgun and wrenched it from Tate's grasp, and in the same movement, delivered a backhanded blow which sent the old rancher reeling to the ground. Blood trickled from Tate's mouth as he gasped, 'Yu scum – what have yu done to him?'

'He's all right, old man,' said the leader. 'He's bein' – taken care of.' He raised his voice.' Ain't that right, Ray?'

'Right,' came a voice from the house.

'Damn yore eyes,' said Tate, weakly, struggling to rise. 'If my boys was around, yu'd—'

'Well they ain't,' snapped the big man with finality. A gesture brought two of the gang to his side. They grasped the rancher firmly by the arms and dragged him to his feet. With an oath, he tossed the shotgun away into the corral, and reached to his saddle horn for the coiled rope hanging there.

He turned to face the old rancher. 'We got a remedy for roosters as crow too much,' he grinned evilly. 'We stretch their necks a mite.'

Meanwhile Green, moving across the back of the ranch house, had rapidly assessed the situation. Unseen by the riders intent on binding Tate's hands and feet, he circled noiselessly around the back of the house and moved silently through the kitchen and into the hallway. There he paused a moment to orient himself with the unfamiliar house. The faint shuffle of a man's feet came startlingly clear. Risking a quick glance around the edge of the door, Green saw the old cook's body sprawled beside the window, half sitting up, and obviously dazed from a blow dealt him by the tall, gangling man who now, his back to Green, was watching the proceedings outside. In one swift, merciless movement, the cowboy leaped across the room and slashed the man Ray across the back of the head, behind the ear, with the barrel of his forty-five. Ray fell like a pole-axed steer, and without a wasted motion, Green stripped the man's belt and gunbelt from his waist and with them tightly bound Ray's hands and feet. A moment or two more sufficed to revive Cookie sufficiently for Green, finger to his mouth to enjoin silence, to thrust Ray's pistol into the cook's hand, and motion him to keep the stunned ruffian covered. Cookie nodded; without a word Green retraced his path out of the house and around the side of the building within a few yards of the tall cottonwood where the four men had thrust Tate roughly into the middle of the horse.

'Any message yu want us to take to our boss, Tate?' jeered the leader, amid the guffaws of his cronies.

'Yu–can–go–plumb–to–hell!' croaked the old man. The man reacted with a curse and swung his arm back to slap the horse across its haunches. His hand never completed its downward movement, for in that split second a shot rang out which spun him backwards on to the ground, cursing and clutching a shattered arm. The other three whirled in the direction from which the shot had come, hands flashing towards their holsters.

'Don't even *think* it,' was the icy warning, and one look at the slit-eyed stranger holding the still-smoking six-shooter was enough to make them jerk their hands away from their weapons as if they had suddenly become red hot.

'First, shuck yore gunbelts. Pronto!' He emphasised the order with a gesture of the six-shooter, and the three men complied rapidly. Green thereupon directed one of them to unbuckle and throw to one side the gunbelt of their wounded leader, who was now sitting upright, nursing his wounded arm and cursing in a steady monotone. In a moment, still keeping the unwholesome quartet covered, Green had stepped beside Tate and with a quick slash of his knife freed the old man's hands. Tate slid easily out of the saddle and flipped a pistol from one of the discarded belts. Then he backed over beside Green.

Meanwhile, the big man had staggered to his feet. His face was white with pain, but he faced his captors without fear. To Green, he said, 'Mister, yo're new in these parts, an' maybe yu don't know what yo're gettin' involved in.'

Green grinned mirthlessly. 'Anyone'd think yu had some kinda ace-in-the-hole.'

'Yo're damned right,' snarled the leader, raising his voice. 'Let him have it, Ray!'

'Ray can't let me have it,' grinned the cowboy. 'I took it off him.' The bantering tone had left his voice when he spoke again. 'Now.' The voice was as flat and menacing as the hiss of a cobra – 'who are yu, mister man, an' who sent yu?'

'I'll tell yu anythin' yu want to know, because tomorrow you'll be dead meat for the buzzards. I'm Bull Pardoe. These others are my men. We call ourselves The Shadows.'

'Sidewinders'd be a better name, I'd say,' Green told him coldly. 'I'm not interested in yore label, Pardoe. Who sent yu?'

'Nobody sent us. We don't run anyone's errands, an' we don't need to.'

'Yu expect me to believe that?' snapped Tate. 'Why yu lyin' scum, I know yo're Barclay's hired hands, so why bother to deny it?'

'Barclay don't own us, mister,' was the vicious reply. 'Nobody owns us.'

'I can see where nobody would want to,' observed Green dryly, 'but me, I wouldn't believe yu if yu told me it was goin' to snow next winter.'

'Then don't ask yore smart questions, stranger. Save yore breath, because when yo're dyin' yu'll need it.'

Green regarded the big man thoughtfully for a moment. He nodded, as if coming to some decision. A quick word with George Tate sent that worthy hurrying up to the ranch house, and in a few moments he reappeared, this time with Cookie, prodding the still-groggy Ray with the worthy's own six-shooter. 'Git on, yu sidewinder,' the cook was snapping, 'an' don't keep all yore sidewinder buddies waitin'. Git!' The order was emphasised by another jab from the gun barrel. The old cook herded the sullen Ray over with the others, then turned to Green with a pleased smile on his face. The cowboy returned his attention to the prisoners.

'Yu made yore play, an' it come unstuck. Yore loud-mouth friend Pardoe has made it plain that lettin' yu go would be a mistake. So I reckon I better kill yu.'

Pardoe faced Green, frowning.

'Yu wouldn't do it.' It was a statement, not a question.

'Nope. I don't reckon I would,' was the reply. 'However since I'm by nature a forgetful man, I'm aimin' to make shore I know yu if we meet up again.'

Without a word, his hand flashed to the left hand holster, and the pistol was talking fire before the watchers had fully appreciated that he had drawn. Each of the gang screeched as the bullets burned furrows along their cheek-bones, nicking the tips of their left ears.

Green regarded the cringing figures before him with distaste.

'Now yu got my mark on yu,' he told them coldly. 'If I

see any o' yu again, I'll start in shootin' without any o' the jawin'.

Wordlessly, the five men turned their horses and pounded away into the darkness now setting like a mist on the valley. Behind Green, George Tate let out his breath in a long whistling sigh. 'Jim, I'm owin' yu—'

'—an extra piece o' that apple pie Cookie promised me?' interrupted Green. 'An' I'm aimin' to take full settlement. Shucks, Mr Tate, I'm glad I was around. Them fellers wasn't joshin' none about stringin' yu up.'

Green and the old rancher walked back towards the porch, and were just settling down in the wicker chairs set on the verandah when, for the second time, approaching horses were heard. Tate rose to his feet and drew his six-shooter. It came as no surprise to him after seeing the man in action that Green was already on his feet, and that the deadly Colts were already in the cowboy's hands, cocked for firing.

'Probably my lads,' Tate told the cowboy, 'but let's make shore.'

In a cloud of dust, five riders swung into the yard and dismounted in the haphazard, careless way of the born rider. One of them, a tall young fellow with the expression of one who has never had anything to hide, tossed his reins to a grizzled old puncher of about fifty, who walked with a pronounced limp.

'Yore turn to be stable boy,' grinned the youngster. 'If yu ain't too tired after racin' the best rider in the valley.'

'That's Dave Haynes,' whispered Tate. 'He's a good kid. The old feller is Gimpy MacDonald – been with me for more years 'n I care to recall. Stove up in a stampede one time, busted his leg up real bad, but he's still a top hand.'

The young man mounted the porch steps still savouring the victory of the race which had meant he didn't have to unsaddle his own horse. His face fell, and mock terror replaced the grin as he caught sight of Tate's drawn gun.

'Hey!' he said, 'I done my chores, boys – honest! How come the reception committee?'

'Dave, quit foolin', an' step over here an' meet Jim Green. Lucky for me he was around. Had a mite o' trouble while yu was gone.'

The others joined them and one by one shook Green's hand, while Gimpy came trudging across the yard, grumbling to himself. Tate introduced the old puncher to Green. Gimpy's eyes flicked quickly over Green's serviceable range gear and the two low-tied guns. He said nothing more than 'howdy', but Green knew he had been weighed and judged by the old timer. Tate meanwhile was busily retailing the events of the preceding hours.

'Yu got any idea who they was, boss?' asked the cowboy who had been introduced by Tate as Ben Dobbs. The old man described the men, especially the leader, to his riders, who one by one shook their heads.

'Never seen anyone around town fittin' them spessyfications,' remarked a pudgy little rider whose sobriquet was Shorty. 'Have yu, Curt?' This to a good looking rider of medium height, whose handsome countenance was spoiled only by a weak mouth which came close to giving his face a permanent sneer. This man, Green knew from the introductions, was Curt Parr.

'Ain't likely we'd see any o' them in town, if they really was the Shadows,' Parr said. 'They shore don't socialise much as I've heard.'

At this point the discussion was interrupted by the arrival of Cookie, who came to the door and stood arms akimbo, with mock – or mostly mock – anger written all over his face.

'Yu fellers gonna stand here jawin' all night? If so, I'll

feed yore supper to the hawgs an' eat the pie myself.'

At this 'invitation' the hungry Slash 8 riders piled into the big dining room and took their places at the big whitewood table, polished by years of use, while Cookie brought in steaming platters of food.

'Let's eat,' said Tate. 'We can talk later.'

The next forty minutes or so were devoted exclusively to the devastation of the fine meal that the cook, despite his ordeal of the afternoon, had rustled together. Juicy steaks, fried potatoes, fresh bread, a formidable driedapple pie, all disappeared like smoke before the combined onslaught of these hardy outdoors-men. Pushing his coffee cup away after the cook had tried to refill it for the fourth time, Green leaned back in his chair with a sigh and reached for the makin's.

'Ridin' the chuck line, Jim?' Tate asked mildly. It was a polite way of asking if Green had a job, or money.

'I ain't broke, if that's what yu mean, seh,' the cowboy told him. 'An' I got a job – sort of.' Green said no more, but many years later, when the news reached them that his 'job' was finished, those present were to remember his words.

Green leaned back in his chair and through the smoke of his cigarette surveyed the Slash 8 outfit as they joshed each other about the day's work. Gimpy, loyal, tough, and incorruptible, one of the old breed of riders who would literally die for the ranch he worked on, was obviously their unofficial leader. Dave Haynes, a straight, open youngster without an ounce of guile in his system. Dobbs and Shorty, both young, both full of high spirits, both likely to be good men to have around when things got tough. Only Curt Parr puzzled him; the man's personality didn't seem to fit in this essentially happy-go-lucky group. Green resolved to ask the old man about Parr later if he got the chance. At that moment, his reverie was interrupted by the rancher himself, who pounded the table with his fist for silence.

'Boys, I ain't much on speechifyin',' the old man began, 'but I got somethin' to tell yu. This is about my girl Grace.'

Gimpy leaned over to Green and murmured. 'The old man's daughter. She's in some fancy school back East.'

'Grace is nigh on twenty-one years old, boys, and she ain't been out here for mebbe ten years. She's been in a high-toned school since I cain't recall when, an' I'm wagerin' she ain't over-interested in running no ranch in New Mexico. I made me a will, years ago, an' if anythin' happens to me, the Slash 8 goes to Grace. Yu boys followin' my drift?'

'Hell, boss, yo're sayin' that if anythin' happens to yu, we'll prob'ly find ourselves riding the chuckline,' Dobbs said.

''That's about the way of it,' Tate admitted.

'Well, only one thing we can do, ain't there?' Gimpy asked. The Slash 8 crew nodded almost in unison. 'Just make dang shore nothin' happens to yu!' finished the old puncher.

A babble of agreement and argument followed these words, until Gimpy pounded the table with the butt of his six-shooter and, casting a cold eye upon his fellows, stood up and announced, 'I just ee-lected myself spokesman for thisyere outfit. Anyone got any complaints about that, now's the time to voice 'em!'

There was a silence worthy of a cemetery, and Green smiled to himself at Gimpy's command over the crew.

'Boss, what we got to say can be said short an' sweet. We-all don't care if yu leave the Slash 8 to the Ol' Ladies Home. Long as yo're here, we aim to stay herewith yu, come hell or high water.'

A shout of agreement followed this speech, and Tate

looked at his riders with an expression in which relief fought against and was extinguished by affection. With misty eyes, the old man said, 'She's a gamble, either way, but I figger the Slash 8's worth it. Them night-ridin' skunks'll have a tough row to hoe.'

'Yu said it, boss,' chimed in Dave Haynes, his eyes snapping with eagerness. 'Give Cookie a gun an' there'll be seven of us. That'll make 'em think twice afore they try anything.'

'Mebbe I didn't oughta butt in on yore private scrap, seh,' interposed Green, 'but yu can make that eight – if yu an' yore boys'll have me.'

Tate looked up quickly. 'Yu mean yu'd – throw in with us, Jim?'

'Why not?' was the cool reply. 'I ain't shore but what I might find what I'm a-lookin' for right here in Sweetwater Valley.'

'Well, dang me if yu ain't welcome, an' that's for true,' Tate chortled. 'We can use all the help we can get.'

Green's eyes flickered quickly over the faces of the Slash 8 crew. In only one pair of eyes did he see anything except wholehearted camaraderie.

When it was time to turn in, Tate asked Dave Haynes to make up an extra bunk for Green in the bunkhouse. Green stood as well, but Tate motioned him to stay, and when they were alone, he faced the new Slash 8 man squarely.

'Jim, how would yu feel about lookin' after my affairs for me – if somethin' was to happen?'

'Mister Tate, yu don't know anythin' about me,' Green told the rancher. 'I'm thinkin' yu feel beholden to me, account o' what happened. But—'

'– but, nothin', Jim. I reckon I know how to size up a man.'

All traces of humour disappeared from Green's face as

he spoke, and something akin to sorrow took its place. 'I'm right proud o' yore confidence. But I better tell yu how wrong yu are: down in Texas, where I come from, I'm known by another name. They call me "Sudden".'

Sudden! Tate's eyes widened at the revelation. So this quietly-spoken young man who had already so ably demonstrated his wizardry with the six-gun was Sudden, who had cleaned out Hell City and Lawless! Few had not heard of his lightning speed on the draw, his amazing adventures, or of the fact that he was wanted for murder. Tate looked afresh at the man who had saved his life.

'Jim,' he said slowly, 'I don't care where yu come from, or what yu done. From here on in, I ain't never believin' another lyin' word I ever hear about Sudden the outlaw.'

'It's true enough, seh,' Green said. 'If I hadn't told yu, it mighta come back on yu some day.'

Tate puffed on his pipe furiously for a moment.

'What I said still goes,' he announced finally. 'If anythin' happens to me, I want yu to run this ranch until my girl is of age. I'm a-makin' a paper tonight to this effect. Tomorrow, I'll send it over to my old friend Judge Amos Pringle in South Bend.' He hesitated a moment. 'I'll have to tell him, boy.'

Green looked up quickly. 'Yu trust him.' It was not really a question, but Tate nodded just the same. 'Then tell him the whole story,' continued Green. The two men sat limned by the lamplight, Tate listening in amazement to the story of a boy's promise to a dying man of a blind search for two killers which had ensued, and of the false accusation that had sent Green, then a mere youth, wandering in the West with a price on his head and every man's hand against him. At the end of the story, Tate shook his head and said, 'What I said goes, Jim. If yo're Sudden, then there's been some damn lies told about yu. In the meanwhile'– he held out his hand – 'I'm backin' yu to a fare-thee-well. Yu'll take the job?'

'I'll do the best I can, seh,' promised Sudden. The two men shook hands gravely.

'Never expected nothin' else,' was Tate's gruff rejoinder.

They said goodnight and Sudden left the old man alone with his pipe in the comfortable room. 'So that's Sudden,' Tate reflected. 'He's all o' that, I reckon. I'm mighty glad he's on my side o' the river.' Nodding to himself, he sat down at the battered old roll top desk, pulling out pen and paper. He scratched away laboriously for some time until what he had written was entirely to his satisfaction, and then walked over to the kitchen door and called for Cookie, who came in wiping his hands.

'Want yu to read that,' Tate nodded at the letter, 'an' witness my signature.'

Without comment, Cookie picked up the letter and read what Tate had written.

'What's this bit mean here?' the cook asked, ' "When Green is ready to tell you about himself, judge him by his actions up to then as you know them and nothing else." '

'It means I ain't tellin' yu no more'n I told Judge Pringle,' was the waspish reply. 'Just sign the letter.'

'I'll sign,' muttered the cook, 'but yo're shore puttin' a lot o' trust in a man yu only met today. He could be planted by Barclay, yu ever think o' that?'

'Shore,' was the equable reply. 'I'm gamblin' on it not being so. In fact, yu might say I was stakin' everything I own on it.'

Cookie nodded, once, then quickly scribbled his signature beneath that of his employer. 'I just hope he ain't gonna get frightened off if things get tougher.'

The old man shook his head his tired eyes bright.

'Somethin' tells me he's a hard man to frighten, Cookie.'

TWO

The little town of Hanging Rock lay torpid under the blasting heat of the summer sun. All along the single street the boardwalks were empty, and only a mangy dog, lying in the ineffective shade of Diego's saloon, gave any indication that there was life in the town. All the citizens of the little cowtown were prudently avoiding the midday heat in the cooler corners of either their own homes or one of the two saloons. A true frontier settlement, Hanging Rock looked like any of a hundred other dusty cowtowns.

Of the various buildings scattered along the street, very few were of any importance. The biggest was Burkhart's saloon and Dance Hall. To everyone except its owner, Burkhart's was known as 'Dutchy's' thanks to the universal western custom of calling anyone with a foreign accent by that sobriquet. Directly opposite Dutchy's was the Traveller's Rest, an hotel and rooming house run by a fiercely independent Irish widow named Mulvaney. Here food and lodging was dispensed for overnight travellers on the stage, or visiting miners, cowboys, and other itinerants. Mrs Mulvaney was a strict disciplinarian and there wasn't a man in the valley who would have dared to walk along one of her highly-polished hallways with his boots on. Down the street a little, on the same side as Dutchy's, stood the City Bank – the most solidly-built structure in Hanging

Rock, and the only one of two storeys.

Adjacent to it was another saloon called 'The Square Deal', but more frequently referred to as Diego's, its owner being a Mexican so named. Most of the cowboys in the valley were traditionally customers of Dutchy's, prior to the arrival of Barclay. His hardbitten crew had, however, taken to frequenting Diego's, which gave Jacob Burkhart no sleepless nights at all. He was a realistic man, and knew that Barclay's men would have given him more trouble than a barrel full of rattlers if they had ever come into the saloon when – say – the Slash 8 boys were in town. In fact, it was Gimpy who had once acidly remarked of Diego's hostelry that 'the only square deal you get there is on the sign outside'.

The rest of the town comprised a pair of general stores, a livery stable with a blacksmith's shop, and the various shacks and dugouts which housed the permanent residents of Hanging Rock.

On this particular day, four men rode into Hanging Rock from the direction of Summerfield, the next town on the road to Santa Fe. The hock deep dust of the street muffled the sound of their horses' hoofs. They looked like four cowpunchers on their way for a drink at Diego's, although it was a rarity to see punchers in off the range so early in the day. An onlooker might have been mildly surprised by the fact that they did not, however, stop outside the saloon, but proceeded to the bank, where they dismounted and hitched their horses. The same onlooker – had there been one – might have been even more surprised to see three of the men go into the bank, leaving one of their number outside with the horses; this man lounged carelessly against the hitching rail, watching the silent street from beneath the shaded brim of his sombrero.

For perhaps eight or ten minutes there was silence, and

then the thunder of a shot shattered the stillness. In the same moment, the door of the bank opened to allow two of the men to back outwards, their shoulders stooped under the weight of heavy satchels. A second or two later, their leader – a big man, solidly built – backed out, a still-smoking six shooter clasped in his meaty paw. With a quick nod to his companions the leader vaulted into the saddle, and in a whirl of dust the four men rode headlong towards the edge of town.

A moment more passed; then a tall, sallow man rushed to the door of the bank, a heavy pistol in his hand, which he emptied in the direction of the fleeing bandits. The fusillade had awakened the dozing townspeople, and men poured from the buildings into the street, running in the direction of the bank, until Hanging Rock resembled nothing so much as a kicked-over anthill. One citizen, late in leaving the welcome coolness of Dutchy's, grabbed the arm of a passer-by and asked a question.

'Four masked men,' shouted his informant, without stopping. 'They just cleaned out the bank an' shot Charley Clark!'

Charley Clark, of course, was well known to the solvent of Hanging Rock as the cashier of the City Bank, and the news inflamed the crowd. There were shouts of 'Let's get after them!' and 'Somebody bring a rope!' as the crowd milled around the steps outside the bank. This clamour was partially stilled by the appearance of the Sheriff of Hanging Rock, who called for posse men to pursue the robbers, and within minutes, had fifty mounted men behind him, ready to ride. With many shouts and oaths, this motley cavalcade swept out of town in hot pursuit of the raiders.

The town's only practitioner of medicine of any sort, an unkempt character who rejoiced in the nickname of 'Patches', was called to minister to the dying Clark. The cashier was promptly taken to a quiet room at the Traveller's Rest, where the curious found Mrs Mulvaney an insuperable obstacle to their attempts to gain more intimate information than could be obtained from those left behind in the now half-empty town's only street.

Some hours later, Brady and his posse returned to Hanging Rock, dusty, saddle sore, and completely unsuccessful. They had trailed the bandits – who had made no attempt to disguise their tracks – in a huge circle out of the town, over the foothills to the north, across the northern part of the Box B – Barclay's range – and to the edge of the rolling Badlands. There, in hock-deep sand and flint-like rock formations, they had lost the trail completely and finally retraced their route to town, arguing hotly among themselves as to the probable destination of the thieves, cursing themselves as fools, and Brady who had led them.

The news of the robbery was relayed to the Slash 8 that evening by Tom Gunther, one of the riders on Mike Mountford's spread over on the far side of South Bend.

'Hell an' damnation, that's bad news,' swore Tate. 'I'm wonderin' what de Witt'll do if he's cleaned out.'

'That's what I rode by to tell yu,' said Gunther. 'Brady's called a meetin' of all the local people for tomorrow afternoon, an' I jest bet myself a dollar de Witt is goin' to be the star speaker.'

Promising to see them in town the next day, Gunther thundered off down the valley with his bad news. Tate turned to face Sudden.

'Jim, I got a feelin' this is gonna be bad for us. If de Witt calls my mortgage now, I'm sunk.'

'Maybe we just oughta wait an' see what this banker fella has in mind,' offered Sudden. 'Don't wanta look on the black side till yu got to.'

Tate's gloom lifted momentarily. 'Maybe yo're right, Jim. Leastways, we can talk to de Witt first, an' worry after we hear what he has in mind.'

'De Witt,' mused the cowboy. 'Unusual handle.'

'Easterner,' agreed Tate. 'Finicky sorta gent, although I ain't sayin' he don't deal square. I never had no reason to complain with either him or Clark.'

Sudden looked his question, and the rancher went on to explain, 'Clark – that's the cashier that's cashed – used to run the bank until de Witt came out here a couple o' years ago. Persuaded Pat Newman, who runs the mines up on Thunder Mesa, to let the bank handle the mine's payroll, which shore brings some extra business into Hangin' Rock. Them merchants down there'd kiss de Witt's boots if he told 'em to.'

'I'm takin' it yu still ain't one of his admirers, though?' hazarded Sudden.

'I can't put my finger on what it is I don't like about the man. I guess I'm just gettin' old an' crotchety.'

To this observation Green made no reply, determining to make up his own mind about the banker at the first opportunity.

Next morning, Sudden and his employer saddled their horses and rode into Hanging Rock. Tate and Sudden plunged into the babel of noise and people that was Dutchy's saloon, and the oldster ploughed his way through the crowd to reach the side of a roly-poly man of middle height, perhaps fifty years of age, whose hair was white at the temples and whose vest was liberally dusted with ashes from the evil-smelling cigar in his mouth.

'Well, here's Tate now,' said the man. 'This is a right howdedo, George. What do you make of it?'

Tate shrugged his shoulders and Sudden asked the group of men whether anyone knew how much had been stolen. 'Twenty thousand, I heard,' answered a nearby man over his shoulder. The roly-poly man looked at Sudden quizzically, and Tate hastened to make the introductions.

'Jim,' he announced, 'thisyere's Mike Mountford, the biggest liar in the Territory.'

'That's takin' in a fair amount of ground,' smiled Sudden. 'Yu must tell a pretty tall story.'

'I never tell nothin' but the truth, boy,' boomed Mountford. 'It's just these small-minded folk around hyar that don't believe it 'less they've seen it with their own peepers.'

'Tales yu tell, I wouldn't believe yu if'n yu told me an ass was an animal with four legs,' grinned Tate, good-naturedly.

'Wal, that's as may be,' Mountford allowed. 'I c'n point to an ass with two legs right about now, however, an' I'm bettin' yu'll believe me.'

He pointed with his chin at a fat, ungainly man using a stool to climb up on the bar – a performance which was not allowed to pass unnoticed by the habitués of Dutchy's bar, who raised a ribald cheer to greet it.

'Our Sheriff,' Mountford told Sudden, 'referred to by those who know an' detest him as "Shady" Brady.'

Sudden watched the fat man's reaction to the jeers of the spectators which accompanied his unedifying scramble on to the bar. The man's weak mouth and piggy eyes revealed his discomfort – and his hatred of – the attentions of Hanging Rock's citizenry.

'Shore looks like a misfit,' he observed to his employer.

'Like I told yu,' nodded Tate. 'If brains was blastin' powder, Shady wouldn't have enough to assassinate an ant.'

They turned back towards the bar as Jake Burkhart, the burly, bearded owner of the saloon, pounded upon the bar with a wooden mallet. After a few moments of this, the noise level dropped sufficiently for the Sheriff's squeaky voice to be heard.

'For them as don't yet know the details,' Brady announced, 'the bank was robbed yesterday by four masked men. They shot Charley Clark, an' cleared off with around twenty thousand dollars in cash.'

One or two awed whistles punctured the silence which followed these words.

'They musta known that the payroll for the mines had arrived. That was the biggest part of the loot. The rest was cash on hand. Mr de Witt'll tell yu all about that later. I raised a posse—'

'– Yu mean it raised yu, don't yu, Sheriff?' called a dry voice from the back of the room, raising general laughter. The discomfited Sheriff cast a black look in the direction from which the jibing voice had come, and went on, 'Like I said, we raised a posse an' trailed the robbers. They took a big wide sweep across the back of town, across the north foothills o' the Needles. That's where we lost 'em. Tryin' to find a trail in that country is as hard as—'

'– Tryin' to get yu to buy a drink!' came the same voice that had previously spoken. Brady whirled towards the direction from which it had come, his hand flying to the gun strapped around his ample middle.

'Yu better watch yore lip, unless yu want to spend a few days in jail,' he shrilled. 'Let's see who yu are, anyway.'

To Sudden's surprise the crowd parted to allow a dishevelled-looking man to step forward.

'Patches, the town medic,' whispered Tate. 'Yu watch Shady back down.'

Sure enough, the appearance of his tormentor had removed all of Brady's bluster. 'Patches', as he was called, was not a figure to inspire this reaction, Sudden thought. Dressed in a frock coat which had once been black and was now a mottled dirt grey, a collarless boiled shirt soiled by months of wear, and greasy corduroy trousers, tucked into the tops of cracked scuffed half boots, the town's doctor looked anything but prepossessing. His chin was unshaven, his eyes bleary, and his voice, when he spoke, was hoarse.

'Well, Shady, my friend, are you going to lock me up?'

Snatching at his only opportunity to save face, Brady snapped, 'Yu know I ain't goin' to lock yu up while yo're sick, Patches. But one o' these days yo're goin' to let that tongue o' yours run a mite too fast, an' when yu do—'

'Oh, step down, you blustering fool!' snapped the doctor, impatiently. 'I'm sure Mr de Witt can make more sense in one sentence than you could if you wrote a book. That,' he finished savagely, 'is always supposing that you can write.'

The Sheriff, with a look of pure hatred for his tormentor, scrambled awkwardly down from the bar.

Hanging Rock's banker, de Witt, was tall and painfully thin, so that even standing erect, his figure seemed hunched. His complexion was yellowish and jaundiced; his hands, bony and clawlike, hung by his sides as if they did not belong to him. Only the dark, deepset eyes were truly alive, watching every movement from beneath low, heavy brows and cavernous eye sockets. The forehead was noble and high, sloping backwards slightly to thick, black, straight hair. The whole figure was dressed in sombre black, relieved only by the white of a good linen shirt.

'Gentlemen,' began the banker, 'I will begin by confirming what you have already heard – that the amount stolen from the bank was twenty thousand dollars in cash. What the Sheriff did not say, and indeed, did not know, was that the amount comprised almost all of the money in the bank.' He held up his hand again to stem the growing swell of speculation that followed this revelation. 'Let me say now, your money is quite safe. Nobody will lose his money. Our head offices can more than guarantee these losses. But I must meet the mine payroll, and to do that I must call in any debts now outstanding to the bank. I am referring particularly to anyone who has short term mortgage loans from the bank. I will not mention any names, as this might be embarrassing for the individuals concerned.'

So saying, he slid down off the bar and pushed his way out of the saloon. The crowd watched him go in silence, and then a veritable avalanche of voices descended into the stillness, while Dutchy and his helpers struggled manfully to comply with orders for drinks at the long bar.

Sudden turned to his employer, who was in conversation with Mike Mountford and a small, compactly-built, efficient-looking newcomer who wore a neat grey suit and soft sombrero. Tate introduced this man as Pat Newman, the manager of the Thunder Mesa silver mines. Newman's face was concerned.

'I'm hoping that de Witt can arrange my payroll quickly,' he was saying. 'I can always bring in some money to pay off the men, but that would mean keeping them without pay for about two weeks. I can always keep them in line, I suppose, but I'd just as soon avoid having to.'

'Well, it looks like my mortgage will be called for shore,' said Tate. 'Damnation, why'd a thing like this have to happen right now? Couldn't come at a worse time. There's just no market for beef anywhere at this time of year, an' I ain't got no other way to raise coin.'

'Wal, thank the Lord I ain't in that kind of bind,' Mike Mountford said slowly, with shrug of his huge shoulders. 'In fact, the bank has coin o' mine. It ain't much . . . but George, if a couple of hundred dollars would help, yo're more than welcome.'

'That's a mighty generous offer, Mike,' Tate said humbly, 'but the truth is that I need much more than a couple o' hundred to pull me outa this hole.'

Struck by a thought, Sudden touched the mine manager's elbow and drew him to one side as Tate and Mountford continued their discussion.

'Just occurs to me, seh,' Sudden told Newman. 'Where do yu buy yore beef?'

Newman looked puzzled for a moment, then said, 'Oh, you mean for feeding the men? I usually buy from Marty Black at South End. Why d'you ask?'

'How many head do yu buy?'

'About five hundred. But look, young fellow, if you're thinking of selling me Slash 8 beef, forget it. I get a very keen price from Marty Black, who's just ten miles away from the mines. He has no problems about delivery and the cows aren't stringy after a tough trail across the Badlands, or through the mountains. I get a full herd, not what's left of a herd when somebody tries to drive through Thunder Ravine.'

Sudden nodded, a slight smile on his face.

'Furthermore,' continued Newman, slightly nettled by the smile, 'Black's price, as I told you, is very keen. It wouldn't be economical to drive cattle to me for the price I pay Black.'

'I'm bettin' yo're wrong, seh,' Sudden said eventually. 'But afore I tell yu why, can I ask yu a favour?' Newman nodded, and Sudden continued. 'I'd like yu to keep what I'm goin' to tell yu to yoreself. Not a word to anyone. Will yu do that?' The mystified mine manager nodded once more.

'I suggest you get to the point,' he put in.

'I'm about to,' Sudden told him. 'Here's my bet: I'm bettin' yu five hundred head o' cattle – or the equivalent in cash – that I can get a herd to yu at the mines in as good a condition as Marty Black can, at the same price yo're payin' Marty Black. If I can't, or if the cows ain't in the condition yu require, I forfeit the herd – or the cash, if yu prefer it. What do yu say?'

'I say you're mad,' snapped Newman. 'It can't be done.'

'It can,' was the quiet reply. 'There's only one condition.'

'Ah,' said Newman quietly, 'a condition. What is it?'

'That you buy the herd within the next ten days.'

Newman studied the man before him. Something about his demeanour suggested that if this man said he was going to do a thing, it would get done. And he knew perfectly well what Tate's rider was up to. If he could sell a herd, there'd be enough money to pay off Tate's debt to the bank. It was a calculated gamble, and one that appealed to Newman.

'Mister Green,' he said with a smile, offering his hand, 'I'll take that bet.'

'Call me Jim,' smiled Sudden. 'An' thanks. Yu just bought yoreself some beef.'

Tate regarded Sudden with mock irascibility when the two rejoined the group.

'Where in thunder yu been, boy?' he growled. 'Yu an' me's got a date with the banker. I guess I'm ornery enough to play the string through to its miserable end, although I know what he's goin' to say. Come on, Jim. Let's get her done.'

THREE

Jasper de Witt was a careful man. His office was a reflection of this fact; it gave no indication of the personality of the man who worked in it, or, indeed, that anyone worked in it at all. There was a huge safe in one corner, a desk, a chair for the banker and two upright chairs for visitors, and a small filing case against the wall. The room had two doors; one admitted visitors from the main part of the bank, while the other led to a stairway which rose to de Witt's personal quarters above the bank.

At the time that Sudden was finishing his arrangements with Newman, the mine manager, the door between de Witt's office and the bank was locked and the blinds were drawn, while a sign hanging outside read 'Back in one hour'. Inside the office, the blinds on the single window were also drawn. Standing facing the seated banker was a huge, hulking brute of a man with a long, evil face scarred down one side by an old knife wound which ran from just below the lobe of the left ear to the corner of the mouth, giving the hatchet face an evil leer.

This was Burley Linkham, foreman of the Barclay ranch; and it was evident from his expression that he was not enjoying this interview.

'When is Barclay due back?' the banker snapped.

' 'Bout a week,' replied Linkham. 'He's stayin' at the—'

'– I know where he's staying,' was the acid comment, 'and with whom. Get word to him to stay where he is until he hears from me.'

Linkham nodded sullenly. 'Something up?'

'One or two things, my friend.' The banker's voice was full of an evil that no one in this town would have ever dreamed existed. De Witt made a steeple of his fingers, pursed his lips, then leaned forward like a striking snake, hissing. 'Give me your feeble excuses for the fact that George Tate is still alive!'

'Hell, boss,' mumbled the discomfited man before him, 'the boys run into some trouble....'

'Bungling fools,' raged the banker. 'I'm surrounded by idiots. As for Pardoe—'

'He's itchin' for another chance at that Green fella,' offered Linkham.

'Is – he – indeed?' ground out de Witt. 'Can you give me one good reason why I shouldn't get rid of Pardoe? I suppose it's lucky that you weren't along. If you had been there, and been recognised, *I would have no further use for you.*' The thinly veiled threat sank in, and Linkham squirmed.

'Hell, it was just pore luck,' he expostulated. 'I'll see that it don't happen again. Yu just tell me what yu want done. I'll tend to it, personal.'

De Witt nodded, as if slightly mollified.

'Thanks to your bungling, I have had to arrange things differently. You had no trouble dodging the posse?'

'Hell, no,' strutted Linkham. 'We had a clear ride to the canyon.'

'And the money?'

'Safe – where you said.'

'Good. The robbery has made it unnecessary for Tate to be visited again by the Shadows. We shall break him financially. It will be just as effective as a bullet. But this stranger who helped Tate is another matter. What do you know about him?'

'Name's Green. Wears two guns an' knows how to use 'em from what the boys said.'

'I want him out of the way,' de Witt said coldly. 'Do you understand me?'

'Don't you worry none,' Linkham assured him. 'I'll take care of it.'

'It might be wiser not to come here for a while . . . afterwards,' said de Witt with an evil smile. He reached into a drawer and brought out a thick roll of bills. Peeling off a number he threw them across the desk.

'Take this for expenses. Pay your men before you do anything else. Money makes silence.'

Linkham nodded, picked up the money and his hat, and de Witt rose and accompanied him to the door. As the big man surveyed the street, de Witt had a final remark to make.

'Don't bungle this, Linkham ... or *I shall act*. Do I make myself clear?'

Shortly after Linkham's departure, the Slash 8 men were ushered into the banker's office with every expression of goodwill. Tate did not beat about the bush.

'De Witt, yo're holdin' a mortgage on the Slash 8. How do I stand?' The banker shifted uncomfortably under the keen gaze of the old rancher, but lifting his chin slightly, as if in defiance, said, 'I regret to say, Mr Tate, that you don't stand too well. I'm going to have to ask you to payoff your debt, or sell your mortgage.'

Tate nodded. 'I figgered that. How long are yu givin' me?'

De Witt was a wonderful actor, and his feelings were rigidly under control, but nevertheless the slightest hint of triumph in the reedy voice did not escape Sudden's sharply attuned ears, and his eyes narrowed as the banker told his employer, 'Not more than ten days, Tate.'

'Ten days!' exploded Tate. 'Damnation, man, yu expect me to raise that kind of money in ten days? Yu got to give me more time than that.'

Tate was also acting a little. On their way to the bank, Sudden had told him about his deal with Pat Newman, so he was playing for a little extra time.

'Ten days is, I might say, extremely generous in the circumstances, Tate,' was de Witt's chill reply. 'Are you telling me that you can raise the money?'

'Yu got me in a tight bind, de Witt,' expostulated Tate. ' got to sell some cattle to raise yore money.'

'I'm surprised to hear that you have a buyer,' said de Witt, artlessly. 'Are you selling in Summerfield?'

'Nope, we got ourselves a buyer— ' Tate began, when his employee cut in and finished the sentence, '— in South Bend. Yu probably know him, seh. Marty Black?'

'No, I can't say I do,' was the banker's reply. He said it without any expression of interest whatsoever. 'You'll be driving across the Badlands? Surely you'll lose too many cattle to make the drive pay?'

Before his employer could open his mouth, Sudden answered again.

'We got no real choice, Mr de Witt. Yu want yore money, an' she's the only way we can figger to raise it.'

'I'm sure that you know what you are doing. Let us hope that you do not encounter these bandits whom Brady tells me have a hideout somewhere in the Badlands.'

'Shucks,' Sudden interposed, 'four of us can handle anything them false alarms care to start. We run 'em off once, an' we can again.'

The unaccustomed bravado in Green's voice made his employer look at him sharply, and his pent-up puzzlement finally overflowed the dam of his judgement.

"Jim, what in the blue blazes—'

'I know, I know, it was supposed to be a secret,' interrupted Sudden, holding up his hand. 'But I didn't figger you meant that Mr de Witt here' – he favoured the banker with an ingratiating smile – 'was included in that. Shucks, if he don't know our plans, he ain't likely to extend our credit.'

George Tate's face set in exasperation at the way that his employee kept forestalling his efforts to speak, but a look which crossed Green's face while the banker's gaze was momentarily averted convinced him that the younger man knew what he was about.

'One thing,' Tate asked. 'How many other debts are yu callin'?'

The banker spread his hands and lifted his shoulders slightly. 'You know I can't tell you that, my friend. A banker is like a doctor – he must respect the confidences of his customers.'

Tate nodded shortly, and rose to leave. De Witt came around from behind his desk to open the door for them. 'You'll be driving pretty soon, then, I take it?' he suggested.

'Pretty soon,' was Sudden's reply, and with it the banker had to be content.

FOUR

The afternoon sun was beginning its slow slide down behind the mountains as George Tate and Sudden left Hanging Rock. Heading along the trail towards the Slash 8, the old rancher said: 'Why for did yu tell de Witt that yarn about the herd? I shore don't recall yore mentionin' any Marty Black buyin' our beef.'

'Neither do I,' grinned Sudden, 'but he exists, which is all that I was concerned with. As it turned out, de Witt had never heard of Marty Black, but I couldn't know that.'

'I don't quite figger all this, Jim. Yu mind tellin' me why our deal with Newman was worth this smoke-screen?'

'Wal, I just had me the hunch in town that the fewer folks know about our plans the less chance there is of anyone puttin' a crimp in them. Now de Witt maybe as honest as the day's long – although my hunch is that he ain't – but a word dropped carelessly can get to the wrong ears just the same as if we posted notices all over the valley advertisin' what we aim to do.'

'Yu shore got me beat,' muttered the old rancher. 'But I allow, I share yore hunch about that banker feller.'

Sudden looked at his employer inquiringly, and Tate continued, 'Yu heard me ask him if he was callin' any other debts?' At Sudden's nod, Tate went on, 'Reason I asked was I know durn well he ain't goin' to pay no mine payroll with my measly couple o' thousand. There ain't no real big operation in these parts exceptin' Barclay that could carry a loan heavy enough to make up the rest o' that twenty thousand dollars. So where would the money come from? An' if there ain't no other loans, then he's callin' my loan for some other reason.'

'How friendly are de Witt an' Barclay?'

'I don't know as I could say. I ain't never heard nothing about them bein' particularly pally. Why'd yu ask?'

'Well, I kind of expected Barclay to be in town today,' Sudden told him.

'I expect he's away again,' Tate said. 'I seen his foreman, Linkham, in town. Usually where yu see one, yu see the other.'

Sudden's line of questioning had put the old man into a deep, thoughtful mood, and they rode along in silence for a few miles. Soon they entered a narrow defile, where tumbled rocks which in past ages had fallen from the towering cliffs of the Needles lay scattered like giant's playthings alongside the trail. He reflected upon their conversation with the banker, and was reviewing what had been said in his mind when his hat was snatched from his head, and the ugly whisper of the bullet blended with the double whiplash-crack of a rifle from the rocks above them.

Reacting without conscious thought, Sudden was out of the saddle and prone on the ground in one fast, flowing movement, and was relieved to see Tate following his example, rolling from the saddle and hitting the dirt solidly a little further ahead.

Levering himself slightly up on his elbows, Sudden whispered to Tate, 'He's up on the rocks, ahead somewhere. Cover me, an'—' He stopped abruptly, with the chilling realisation that the old rancher had not stirred since falling from the saddle, in what Sudden had assumed was an evasive action. He now divined the reason, and wormed his way forward to where the old man lay. He could hear the old rancher's stertorous breathing while he was still a couple of yards away; when he reached the spot, he found Tate lying face downward in the dirt. Sudden turned the old rancher over. Blood drenched the front of Tate's shirt, and the old man's face was grey and drawn in the half light. Sudden had looked upon Death many times; the old rancher had not long to live. He lifted Tate's head gently, and the rancher opened his eyes.

'Take it easy, old-timer,' murmured the cowboy. 'I'll get you some water.'

'No ... don't go!' Tate grabbed Sudden's shirt sleeve urgently. 'Want ... to ... tell ... yusome ... thin'.'

'Hell, it can wait,' said Sudden, through gritted teeth. 'I got to get yu to a doctor.'

'Wastin' ... yore ... time.' Tate managed a faint grin. 'Jim ... the ranch.'

Alarm and worry erased the pain momentarily from the lined old face.

'Don't yu worry now about the ranch. I'll take care of things,' Sudden assured him.

'Pringle ... knows ... our deal.' The old man sighed; a trickle of blood coursed from his grey lips. He struggled to sit up, his eyes wide. 'Grace ... take care....'

'Shore,' Sudden told him softly. 'I'll take care o' Grace. Rest easy, ol' timer. I got to get yu home.'

'Home.' A sigh escaped the old rancher's lips, and with an imperceptible movement, his body slowly relaxed in Sudden's arms. The cowboy let Tate's head slowly and gently down to the ground, knowing that the old man was dead. Sudden's lips were compressed into a thin line, and his eyes were the colour of arctic seas. With a deft movement, he drew his guns, and eased away from the body.

A quick glance around; then he moved slowly forward, scanning the surrounding rocks to check whether the ambusher had moved down nearer the trail for a second attempt. Everything was deathly still. The cowboy nodded to himself.

'I got a hunch Mister Bushwhacker is gone,' he told himself, 'but there's only one way to be shore.'

So saying, he stood upright, poised for an instant dive to the shelter of the shadowed ground. No shot greeted the daring exposure of his unprotected body, and he stood for a moment, lining up angles and distances. Off to the right, a very faint path, running at almost right angles to the trail, offered a possibility, and he moved on silent feet towards it. For perhaps another fifty yards he thrust this way through the fringe of brush and jumbled rocks, and eventually straightened up with a sigh. Here was the place he had been seeking.

Shadowed by a twisted juniper tree, and screened from below by the bushes, was flat rock which bore several scratches, and a soft small thread of red cotton caught on a protruding flint. Two indentations in the soft earth had been caused by the toes of the ambusher's boots as he lay prone on the rock watching the trail. Lying in the same position, Sudden could see the trail clearly, and the two horses cropping the grass not far from the sprawled body of George Tate.

'Easy as A-B-C,' he told himself.

A dull gleam of metal caught his eye, and he stooped quickly. From a crevice between the rocks he fished out a cartridge shell.

'Remington repeater – they ain't so common.'

Nearby he found hoofmarks where a horse had been tethered, and followed the horse's tracks until they reached the main trail and were lost in the churned multitude of tracks. Knowing it would be impossible to track the killer further, he retraced his steps, and was back beside his own horse when the thunder of approaching hoofs sent him fleetly into a shadowed cleft beside the trail where he waited, guns drawn and cocked.

Within moments, Dave Haynes and Gimpy thundered into the clearing around a bend in the trail, pulling their horses into a rearing halt as they saw the sprawled figure on the ground, and the crouched menacing form of Sudden.

'We was in the north pasture,' explained Dave, 'an' we heard shots. We come a'runnin'!'

'Pity yu couldn't have got here about ten minutes earlier,' remarked Sudden, grimly, as a muffled oath came from Gimpy, who had dismounted and was kneeling by George Tate's body.

'Hell's flames, the old man's cashed. Who done it, Jim?'

'I didn't get a look at him,' Sudden admitted. 'We was sittin' ducks.'

He recounted the circumstances of the ambush, and the details of his discoveries in the rocks above.

'Well, there's plenty o' red shirts around these parts, so that's no help. But there can't be many Remington repeaters hereabouts.' Gimpy's voice was flat with anger. 'Let's start by ridin' over to the Barclay spread an' askin' some leadin' questions.'

'Now that'd be plumb foolish, not to mention dangerous,' Sudden said mildly. 'No, I'm thinkin' we'll keep our bushwhackin' friend's Remington a secret for a while. No use tippin' our hands.'

'Shucks, yo're right, of course,' admitted Gimpy. 'I kinda lost my wool for a minnit, Jim – seein' the ol' man like this....'

'I know,' Sudden said gently. 'Yu been with him a long time.'

Gimpy shook his head and did not answer, but brought the rancher's horse across and threw his own saddle blanket across Tate's saddle. The grisly task of roping the old man's body to his saddle was accomplished in grim silence, a silence not broken by any of them the whole way back to the Slash 8.

FIVE

The next morning, Sudden despatched Gimpy to Hanging Rock with instructions to send a telegram to Tate's daughter in New York and to inform the sheriff of the murder of the old rancher.

'Tell him we want a full inquiry,' he instructed Gimpy.

'That fat fool,' growled the old cowboy. 'He couldn't even spell the word.'

An hour or two later, Tate's tarpaulin-covered body was laid gently in the buckboard, driven by Cookie, and the Slash 8 headed in Gimpy's wake.

Sudden had already specified that Burkhart's saloon should be the place for the inquiry to be held. It was to this destination that the Slash 8 contingent now came with their sad burden. As they pulled up alongside the saloon, Sheriff Brady came huffing along the boardwalk.

'Move outa the way, there!' he puffed self-importantly. 'Stand back, now! Make room, there!'

'An' plenty of it,' jibed one bystander. 'Shady shore ain't no mannykin!'

This slighting reference to his bulk brought a flush to the Sheriff's face, but he affected to ignore it as he settled himself at a table to the left, facing the Slash 8 men, while a hastily sworn coroner's jury of sheepish Hanging Rock citizens took their places in chairs immediately to his right. The sheriff's piggy eyes grew narrower as he noticed the prominently displayed weapons of the Slash 8 crew.

'Yu fellows aimin' to attend an inquiry or start a war?' he called.

'Take yore pick, Shady,' retorted Gimpy. 'We'll as lief have one as the other, if yu want to start the ball.'

The sheriff rewarded this remark with a withering glance which had absolutely no effect whatsoever upon the recipient; Brady thereupon grabbed Dutchy's wooden mallet and banged on the table in front of him.

'This meetin's called to order,' he bellowed. 'We're here to discover how the deceased, George Tate o' the Slash 8, met his death.'

'He was murdered,' Sudden informed him coldly. 'What we're here for is to get the facts o' the murder on record.'

'Yu say he was murdered, mister,' retorted Brady. 'We've only got yore word for it.'

A murmur of interest arose from the watchers, but it was stilled in a moment as Sudden, his eyes as cold as polar ice, leaned forward and asked very quietly, 'Yu suggestin' I'm a liar, Sheriff?'

Once again the sheriff's face lost its colour, resembling at this moment nothing so much as a discarded lump of putty.

'I ain't called nobody nothin',' he squeaked. 'I'm only pointin' out that we can't assume any fac's until we've established them here.'

'I think we can safely assume that Tate didn't shoot himself in the back.'

This interruption came from Patches. The town doctor's dry voice effectively silenced anything further that Brady might have been about to say. The doctor had been kneeling beside Tate's body during the exchange between Brady and Sudden; he stood now regarding the sheriff with studied contempt. 'If you are quite ready?'

'Let's have it, Patches,' snapped the lawman impatiently. 'Yu–' this to a meek looking man sitting to one side – 'make notes.' The little man nodded emphatically, and bent over the notebook balanced on his knees. The doctor regarded Brady without expression. 'What do you expect to be told? Tate has been dead perhaps twenty but not less than twelve hours. He was shot from above and behind – which seems to be a fairly common method of killing people in these parts – and probably died within a few minutes of being shot. I would say that he was killed by a rifle bullet of medium calibre. Since the bullet hit bone inside the body it is impossible to say what make of rifle fired the fatal shot. Here is the slug.'

With a disdainful gesture, he tossed a misshapen piece of lead on to the table in front of the Sheriff, and proceeded to wipe his hands upon a large and none too clean rag, produced from one of the capacious pockets of the rusty frock coat. He then turned his back on Brady and the entire proceedings, and poured himself a liberal drink from the bottle which Jake Burkhart had placed in readiness upon the bar.

Brady meanwhile examined the bullet carefully, as though he were appraising a diamond, turning it over in his hands, squinting at it. 'Patches is right,' was his verdict. 'Prob'ly a forty-four, an' purty near every gun in the Territory is the same. I'm guessin' this won't give us no leads.' He passed the bullet across to the jurors who examine it closely, shaking their heads. Brady called Sudden forward.

'Yu was the last man to see George Tate alive. Suppose yu give us yore version o' what happened.'

Sudden thereupon recounted once again the bare

details of the bushwhacking, the search he had made, and the arrival of the Slash 8 men. The only thing he left out was the discovery of the cartridge case. When he had finished Brady stood up and faced him.

'Yu say the last thing George Tate said was that yu should take care o' the ranch an' his daughter, Grace?'

'That's right,' Sudden told him.

'Yet yu've on'y been here a few days yoreself, Green. How come Tate put so much trust in yu?'

'He needed someone to keep the ranch runnin' until his daughter can get here from the East. I'll stay in charge until she's twenty-one. That's what Tate told me.'

A murmur of surprise ran around the room at this revelation, and Brady's pig eyes gleamed.

'Yu shore got yore hands on a good ranch, one way or the other,' he leered.

'What the devil for?' interposed a biting voice. Brady wheeled to discover Patches regarding him with cold eyes, elbows propped behind him on the bar. 'Assuming that Green killed Tate – which only a complete fool would believe for a second – what would he want the ranch for?'

Brady's eyes rolled around the room, seeking some kind of support, for in truth, he had no idea how to answer the question his nemesis had posed.

'How in 'ell do I know?' he squealed. 'This feller had a motive, an' for all I know, seein' he was alone with Tate, bumped him off, intendin' to sell the ranch. . . .' His voice tapered off as the stupidity of what he was saying seeped through his muddled brain.

'That's right – *think*!' came the jeering voice from the bar. 'Green just told us the place is mortgaged. Do you know anyone – apart from a congenital idiot like yourself – who would be willing to buy a mortgaged ranch, Sheriff?'

In the laughter which followed this remark, Brady

struggled visibly to regain his composure. Looking around the room, his eyes fell upon the banker, de Witt, who was standing inconspicuously at the rear.

'Mr de Witt,' called the sheriff. 'Can yu confirm that the deceased's ranch was mortgaged the way this feller says?'

The banker's dry voice was flat and unemotional. 'He had a mortgage. The amount of it is of no concern here, I think. I have one suggestion to make to this inquiry, however.'

Every head in the room turned towards him.

'Has it occurred to anyone that these bandits in the mountains might be responsible for George Tate's death?'

'The Shadows?' Brady's voice was high pitched. 'Why should they want to kill George Tate?'

'I understand that he had been threatened by some masked men, and that he and Green had run them off his ranch. They may have decided to take their revenge by bushwhacking both men. I congratulate you, Mr Green, on your escape.'

Brady pounced upon this idea like a terrier upon a rat. 'It's shore a possibility,' he said. 'I didn't know yu'd had a run-in with the Shadows, Green. Why wasn't it reported to me?'

Sudden lounged back against the table, a faint smile on his face.

'Well, to tell yu the truth, Sheriff, yu was so busy chasin' the Shadows for robbin' the bank, it hardly seemed worth while me tryin' to get them arrested for threatenin' the Slash 8.'

Again the unfortunate lawman suffered the torment of laughter at his expense, but he banged on the table with his mallet and finally achieved order. 'This puts a new light on thisyere killin',' he announced. 'I'm wagerin' that these jurymen here are goin' to agree that George Tate prob'ly met his death by ambush at the han's of one or more o' the Shadows, an' that the motive for the murder was revenge.'

He turned to the men behind him, and held a whispered colloquy with a lanky citizen evidently serving as jury foreman. Then, 'Unless anyone has any new evidence to present, this jury finds – as I expected – that George Tate was prob'ly murdered by the Shadows.'

He whirled to face the Slash 8 contingent. 'Yu fellers are the most concerned in this: do yu disagree with the findin's o' this jury?'

'Let's put her this way,' Green said coldly. 'She's the only verdict we got. Personally, I wouldn't take yore jury's word for what time it was.'

Brady pounded the table with his mallet, and when a small lull in the babble of talk came, he yelled, 'Unless anyone's got further evidence to offer, this hearin's officially closed.'

Sudden watched his departure with distaste, and turned to Gimpy and Dave once more.

'I can shore see why that Patches feller don't like Brady,' he remarked.

'Patches don't like anybody much,' was Gimpy's reply, 'but he ain't skeered to speak his mind, which is more than most o' the folk in this town do. He says what he thinks – every time.'

Sudden nodded, and then, acting upon an impulse, walked over to the bar and joined the doctor. On closer inspection it was evident that Patches' decrepit appearance was largely due to neglect of his clothes and personal hygiene; Sudden put the man's age at no more than forty-five.

'I'd admire to buy yu a drink, seh,' he offered, 'an' thank yu for backin' me up before.'

'Brady is quite detestable, Mr Green,' replied Patches,

'but I spoke up because I am a believer in the truth, and not because of any feeling of sympathy for you or for the Slash 8. I have no time to waste upon sympathy.'

'Men with a quest rarely do have,' said Sudden. The effect of this upon the doctor was electric. He stood upright, his drink slopping over the rim of the glass and on to the bar, while his eyes fastened upon Green's with a terrible intensity. His shaking left hand grabbed Sudden's shirt front, and in a croak, he said, 'What do you mean by that?'

'Shucks, yo're not a drunk, an' yo're not a bum,' Sudden told him. 'That means yo're either disguised or else yu got side-tracked by the drink. I did myself, one time. Yu just have to quit drinkin', doctor.'

The man looked at the cowboy for a long, long moment, but then his eyes fell, and he shook his head violently, a shudder racking the bony frame.

'Changin' the subject,' Green said, as though none of this had taken place, 'Did the bank cashier say anything afore he died?'

'Nothing.' Patches spoke from some far off place, a light gradually coming back into his eyes as he seemed to focus properly upon Green again. 'Why do you ask?'

'To tell yu the truth, I had a hunch that he might have held the key to who these Shadow *hombres* are. He must have recognised one o' them. I figger he was shot to keep him quiet.'

'You are unusually perspicacious, Mr Green. Have you any other theories?'

'A few,' Sudden grinned. 'I'll tell yu about them some time.'

Patches nodded. 'Do that, Mr Green, do that. And while you are theorising, ask yourself this question: how did banker de Witt know the Tate's ranch had been visited by the Shadows?'

'I been askin' myself that already,' Green told him with a grin.

'And so have I, Mr Green. Good day, sir.'

SIX

Every second Thursday, weather and road-agents permitting, the stagecoach between Santa Fé and Las Cruces rolled into Hanging Rock on its way south. The driver, known locally as 'Rye' Johnson because of his predilection for that particular brand of painkiller, cursed his team up the street shortly after two o'clock on the Thursday following the funeral of George Tate. Pulling the horses to a sweating halt in a huge cloud of dust, Johnson slammed on the long handbrake, leaped down from his perch high up on top of the coach, and threw open the door nearest to the boardwalk.

'Hangin' Rock, an' right on time!' he yelled. 'Thirty minnits stop for grub an' a change o' horses!'

'Rye' Johnson was not a man to let ceremony stand in the way of his own thirst, and so, without another word, he left his passengers to unload themselves and their luggage and tramped heavily into the welcome shade of Dutchy's, outside whose saloon the stage always stopped. The usual crowd hanging around the verandah of Dutchy's to watch the arrival of the stage wasted little time watching him, however. Their attention was fixed now upon the man getting out of the coach, which swayed beneath his solid weight. All in all, he gave the appearance of wealth and power combined with a forcefulness which was enhanced by his sheer size. His dark-browed face was now, however, smiling fulsomely for the benefit of a small, pretty blonde girl to whom he had turned in order to help gallantly from the stagecoach. She looked to be in her early twenties.

'Thank you,' she said, smiling, 'for all your kindness. It would have been a dull journey without your company, Mr Barclay.'

'Pleasure's all mind, Miss Tate,' replied Barclay with a deep bow. 'I'm hoping you'll call me Zack, an' that I'll see a lot more of yu while yo're here.'

The girl flushed slightly at the eager warmth in the big man's voice, a pleasant sight which Barclay missed completely having turned to a bystander. Snapping his fingers he rapped, 'You! Take the lady's bags across to the hotel!' Unfortunately for Barclay, however, the man he addressed so contemptuously was none other than the ramrod of the Slash 8, who had ridden into town with Dave Haynes upon receiving Grace Tate's telegraphic communication that she would be arriving on the stage. Barclay was apprised of his mistake when a cold voice cut in upon his gallant attentions towards the young woman.

'Yu may think yo're king o' the valley, mister, but I ain't one o' yore serfs!'

Barclay wheeled in amazement upon hearing this cutting remark, and, since he had never seen Sudden before, ejaculated, 'Who the devil are yu?'

'Well, I'll give you a hint: I ain't one o' yore admirers,' came the reply. Without another word, the Slash 8 man shouldered past Barclay and presented himself, hat in hand, to the young woman.

'Ma'am, my name's Jim Green. I'm runnin' the Slash 8. I brung out a buckboard to take yu back to the ranch as soon as yo're ready, but I figgered yu'd probably want to eat first, an' freshen up some, so I made arrangements at the hotel.' He pointed with his chin across the street, and finished with a smile, 'Anyway, yu call the shots.'

Grace Tate regarded him coolly for a long moment, and then over his shoulder caught sight of the smouldering visage of Zachary Barclay. Not wishing to commence her acquaintance with Hanging Rock by being involved in a street brawl, Grace Tate sought to pour oil on the waters by laying a hand on Sudden's arm and saying, 'Thank you, Mr Green, but I did promise Mr Barclay that we would lunch together. Perhaps you would call for me later at the hotel?'

As Sudden turned to go, Barclay laid a detaining hand on Sudden's arm.

'Just a minute, you!' he snapped.

'Take yore paw off me,' warned Sudden, and the ice in his voice made Barclay snatch away his hand as if the cowboy's arm had suddenly produced a charge of electricity. Involuntarily, he backed away from the wicked gaze that the Slash 8 man bent upon him, and before he could gather his wits to say something, Sudden had pushed through the crowd and into Dutchy's saloon.

For a moment, the watchers thought that the big man might have an apoplectic fit, so suffused with rage did his face become. The drummer who had arrived on the stage gazed reflectively at the width of Zack Barclay's shoulders as the Box B man escorted Grace Tate across the dusty street to the Traveller's Rest. 'I sure wouldn't want to tangle with him,' he breathed.

'Don't yu – ever!' was the salty advice.

The drummer's gaze now swung towards the ramrod of the Slash 8, who was leaning against the bar talking quietly with Dave Haynes and Dutchy. Noting the two low-tied guns, the slim hips, the broad shoulders and whipcord build of the man, the drummer shook his head.

'Now what?' asked his neighbour.

The drummer nodded towards where Sudden stood.

'Just thinkin',' he said. 'I wouldn't want to tangle with *him*, neither.'

Later that afternoon, Dave and Sudden dismounted in front of the hotel and walked into the neat hallway, where a small handbell stood on a counter. Dave lifted the bell and its tinkle elicited a response from the rest of the house, where an Irish brogue shrilled the news that Mrs Mulvaney was on her way out, indeed.

'David,' she beamed, when she saw her visitors. 'Shore an' you've been neglectin' me lately. Why didn't you come in for lunch?'

'He kinda lost his appetite, ma'am,' suggested Green.

'An' we've had our troubles, Mrs M.,' added Dave.

The good lady's face saddened. 'Shore an' it's sad I was to hear of George Tate's murther,' she told them. ''Twas a sad day for this town when that happened.' She paused for a moment. 'Nor did I think I'd live to see the day when a Tate broke bread with a Barclay – beggin' your pardon, David, an' that of your friend.' She looked inquiringly at Dave, who hastened to introduce Sudden.

'Thisyere plug-ugly derelict's named Jim Green, Mrs M.,' Dave told the landlady. 'He claims to be ramroddin' the Slash 8, but I give yu fair warnin' – cards make him reckless, liquor drives him mad, an' if yu give him credit he'll leave town the next mornin'.'

'Right,' snapped the widow, with mock severity, 'I'll treat him just the same as the rest of you Slash 8 bhoys an' it's not far wrong I'll be goin'.'

She bustled away into the rear, leaving the two men exchanging glances of amusement. A few moments later, Grace Tate appeared in the doorway of the hotel dining room, Zachary Barclay close behind her. Bidding her goodbye, the big man bent low over her hand and murmured something.

'Thank you again, Mr Barclay,' Grace Tate said. 'You have been most kind and helpful, and I shall not forget it.'

With a ferocious glare at the two Slash 8 men, Barclay pushed past and went out into the street. Grace Tate came forward and held out her hand to Dave.

'You *must* be David Haynes,' she exclaimed. 'My father wrote so much about everyone at the ranch that I feel I know you already.'

Dave's honest face grew fiery red, and he mumbled something as he took her hand and shook it as though it might bite. Grace Tate then half-turned to face Sudden.

'And you are James Green. I am told that you are a gunfighter, Mr Green.' Sudden, who had not missed the fact that Grace Tate had not extended her hand to him, shrugged, regarding her quizzically.

'I'd say that would depend on who was telling yu, Ma'am,' he said quietly.

The girl lost her poise for a moment, then, regaining control, said, 'I do not imagine, on the basis of what I have heard, that your association with the Slash 8 will continue much longer, Mr Green.'

To this Sudden made no reply, but Dave stared at the girl dumbfoundedly.

'Yu – yu can't mean that, ma'am?' he managed to say.

'I both can and do,' asserted Grace Tate.

'But Jim here—' began Dave, when the girl cut off his protests by saying, 'We can discuss it later at the ranch. I would like to go there immediately if that is possible. I have been informed about the situation in the valley, and of the circumstances of my father's death. I don't want your sympathy—' She held up her hand as Dave opened his mouth. 'The only thing I regret is that I was not here for the funeral.'

'I'm surprised yu got here this quick,' Sudden remarked.

'So am I,' was the cold reply. 'Communications in this Godforsaken land seem to be even more primitive than I remember. However, my main reason for being here is to put an end to all this trouble over Sweetwater Valley.'

'How yu proposin' to do that, ma'am?' asked Dave, with some wonder in his voice.

'I intend to sell the ranch, of course – as soon as I can arrange it.'

Dave looked at the girl before him like a caveman looking at a railroad engine, but before he could speak, Sudden suggested that they go and bring the buckboard so that Miss Tate could ride out to the ranch.

'Bring a saddled horse,' she told them. 'I haven't forgotten how to ride. Just give me ten minutes or so to change my clothes.'

Sudden nodded, while his companion, still regarding the girl with awe, gulped noisily. Wordlessly the two men headed for the door.

'Aw, don't yu worry none, Li'l Breeches,' he told Dave. 'I'm bettin' she's got some o' her paw's blood in her, which is why her dander is up. When she knows the full story, she'll be a mighty different gal. Now why don't you head for the livery stable an' rustle up a hoss. I'll meet yu over at Dutchy's.'

Dave nodded again. 'Jim,' he began, 'I'm sorry I blew my stack. Yo're right, o' course. An' now that yu mention it, she is kinda pretty, ain't she?'

'Not that I recall mentionin' it,' Sudden grinned mischievously, 'but she is.'

He grinned hugely as Dave flushed a deep scarlet and hurried away towards the livery stable, while Sudden descended from the hotel porch to where his horse stood at the hitching rail.

'Looks like he's smitten, Thunder,' he told the horse. 'Or is it smote?'

The black stallion bent a graceful head and nipped playfully at the foot in the stirrups.

'Yu, too?' grinned Sudden. 'I shore am friendless today.'

While Sudden and Dave Haynes had been meeting the new owner of the Slash 8, Zachary Barclay had made his way directly to the bank, where Jasper de Witt was awaiting him.

'You took your time getting here,' was de Witt's waspish greeting.

'I had a piece o' luck,' Barclay told the banker eagerly. 'When I was in the stage office at Santa Fé buyin' my seat, who walks in but Tate's girl, just arrived from New York an' in a tearin' hurry to get to Hangin' Rock. I made shore she got on the same stage as I did.'

'Grace Tate is here, hm?' mused de Witt. 'Yu spent the entire journey in her company?'

'Every mile o' the way,' was the proud reply. 'I shore filled her ear. Good job yu sent me word o' how things was back here.'

'And she swallowed it all?' de Witt's voice was not as enthusiastic as Barclay had hoped, but he plunged on.

'Hook, line, and sinker,' he boasted. 'I just left her at the hotel. She's already agreed with me that the best way to stop trouble is to prevent it. She told me she aims to talk to her lawyer an' fix a price. Then she'll sell the Slash 8 to me. What do yu think o' that?' He clapped his meaty hands on his hips and regarded his master with an air of triumph. De Witt's expression did not alter, and Barclay's pose gradually crumpled. 'What ... what is it?'

'I'm just wondering how you are going to talk that Slash 8 foreman into selling, now that you've got the girl convinced, ' de Witt said.

'Yu tellin' me the girl ain't got the right to sell?' gasped Barclay.

'Damned right I am,' snapped the banker. 'She hasn't got the right to cut the grass on that place without Green's approval.'

Barclay was silent at this revelation. Another idea came to him. 'But yu got the mortgage on the place,' he reminded the banker. 'Yu've foreclosed, ain't yu?'

'That's true, but I won't be able to if Green fulfils his deal to sell a herd in South Bend. If he does, he can pay off his debt, and we have no hold on the Slash 8.'

Barclay smiled evilly. 'I reckon we can put a crimp in his plans.'

'That's what Linkham told me,' snarled the banker. 'He was supposed to take care of this Green fellow. Instead of which, he shot George Tate. There was no need to kill Tate – I had him over a barrel. But Green is still around. I don't see him looking particularly worried about the fact that he's supposed to be dead.'

'If I'd been here, things woulda been different,' Barclay told the banker.

'I seriously doubt that,' came the biting reply, 'but you'll get your chance. In the meantime' – he leaned forward in his chair – 'what did you find out in Kansas City?' Barclay's face broke into a conspiratorial leer, and he leaned forward on the desk.

'You was right, Seth—' he began, but stopped in sheer terror as a look of demoniac rage came into the banker's face. For the second time in the day, Barclay stepped back, flinching as though expecting a blow. He was a big man, and could handle himself well in rough and tumble street fighting, but the cold menace of de Witt's gaze turned his muscles to water.

'Damn you for a loudmouthed fool!' screeched the banker. 'If I ever hear you use that name again I'll slit out your tongue and feed you to the buzzards personally.'

Barclay stuttered and held up his hand as though to

ward off a blow.

'Hell ... I didn't even realise I'd said it ... Jasper, I'm plumb sorry ... it won't happen ... again. For God's sake, Jasper. It was a slip of the tongue.'

'Let it be the last,' snarled de Witt, 'Mister – Barclay.' He paused significantly on the name. 'Your real name spoken, even in this town, would get you hanged in an hour, so never forget yourself. If you speak that name again, you will die – very slowly.'

The cold eyes bored into Barclay's, and the big man said nothing.

'Now – what did you discover in Kansas City?'

Barclay smiled like a human imitation of a cringing, beaten dog who now sees the hand of friendship once more extended.

'Like I said,' he told the banker eagerly, 'yu was right. The surveyors will be movin' along the proposed route in about a month. They'll start buildin' the rail—'

'Damn your eyes, keep your bull voice down!' hissed de Witt. 'Do you want to share your pickings with every derelict in Hanging Rock?'

Barclay longed to reach across the desk with his huge hands and choke the life out of that scrawny neck. But he knew, and the banker knew that he knew, he would never do it. De Witt's hold upon him was too strong, and he knew that his evil master would have placed proofs of Barclay's identity where they could be easily found should he be killed.

'So.' De Witt was silent for a moment. Then, 'You, my over-sized friend, get out of here and be ready to move whenever Green starts that herd towards South Bend. Stop the herd. Stop Green, too. Permanently, do you hear? With Green gone, the girl will have no choice but to sell.'

Barclay nodded again. His face was still sullen, and his soul burned with hatred of this man, who had so mercilessly tongue-lashed him. 'Anythin' else?'

'Be silent,' de Witt told him, 'and I'll make you rich. Remember that.' Barclay knew that he was dismissed. Still seething, he stumbled out into the street. The hot, bright sunlight brought him back to reality after the evil gloom of the banker's office, but his tormented ego knew no peace. Zachary Barclay wanted something or someone to hurt, break, or destroy. It was at this moment that his narrowed eyes descried, preparing to mount a black stallion outside Dutchy's saloon, the ramrod of the Slash 8. Zachary Barclay lengthened his stride.

SEVEN

'Fine horse.'

Sudden looked around to see Zachary Barclay, leaning casually against one of the uprights supporting the verandah roof. The Box B owner's dour visage gave no hint of the fires raging within him.

Sudden nodded, and swung into the saddle.

'I'll give yu a hundred dollars for him.'

'Nope,' replied Green. 'He ain't for sale.'

Several loungers outside Dutchy's had heard Barclay's offer and the Slash 8 man's refusal. Three or four of them drifted nearer to hear the exchange better.

'Two hundred,' insisted Barclay, his face darkening, and when Green again shook his head, 'Three.'

The word had spread rapidly into the saloon, and a small crowd was forming. Even in a country where good horseflesh was money on the hoof, three hundred dollars was a lot to pay. When Green shook his head once more, a sound not unlike a sigh escaped the onlookers.

'Four hundred, then, damn yu!' snapped Barclay. 'That's more than yu an' the horse together are worth!'

Green's lips tightened, and a wintry look was in his eyes.

'I told yu,' said Sudden coldly. 'The horse ain't for sale.'

Barclay frowned. This wasn't going the way he had intended it to. He had offered the man well over half a year's top wages; there were few who would have refused such an offer, no matter how attached they were to their mounts.

'Name yore own price, then,' he cried. 'I aim to have that horse.'

Sudden regarded Barclay sourly for a moment, and then, as if coming to a decision, slid out of the saddle to the ground. Barclay experienced a flush of relief. Evidently it had been just a question of more money – it usually was.

'Yo're sellin', then,' he cried triumphantly.

'Not exactly,' said the Slash 8 man. Barclay's expression of triumph turned to one of bewilderment as the cowboy, holding the reins in his hand, told him, 'I'll make yu an offer. If yu can ride him for five minutes, he's yores – free.'

This surprising counter offer aroused a buzz of comment among the spectators, for it was a sporting one, and Barclay, hearing it, knew he could not back down. With an expansive gesture, he stepped forward.

'Yo're on, Green!' he laughed. 'But Zack Barclay accepts gifts from no man. When I ride him, I'll pay yu what I offered.'

He had no sooner placed himself alongside the horse, however, when the animal whirled, teeth bared, and a vicious snap missed Barclay's arm by a fraction of an inch. With a curse, the big man jumped hastily back, casting a venomous glance at the unperturbed Green. A snicker of laughter trailed from the crowd. 'Ten to one Barclay gives the hoss back!' offered one wag.

A flush of crimson stained Barclay's face and neck as these words reached his ears, and with a lightness not normally to be expected in so big a man, he sprang into the saddle and clapped his feet into the stirrups in one swift movement. A gasp of admiration escaped the watchers, but hardly had the sound escaped their lips when the black stallion squealed with rage and instantly became a fury of activity. Up into the air it leaped, once, twice, thrice, in as many seconds, coming down on legs as rigid as tempered steel, twisting and arching its body from side to side in mid-air, never allowing the rider on its back to recover from one shock to the next. In moments, Barclay's left foot was out of its stirrup, then his right, and finally, within seconds, it was over. The big man reeled backwards, legs horizontal with the ground, and fell like a sack of sand. The enraged stallion whirled around, rearing high, eyes rolling and flailing hoofs ready to strike the puny man-thing lying beneath it when its owner, shedding the air of indolence with which he had viewed the unequal contest between man and beast, sprang forward. With a word, he brought the mighty stallion down to a standstill, and then, talking quietly close to its ear, led the horse back to the hitching rail, the muscles along its flanks and haunches still flickering nervously. The crowd parted rapidly to give the horse plenty of room at the rail, and in the stunned silence not one pair of eyes looked at Barclay.

The owner of the Box B lay where he had fallen. Nobody came to help him. A trickle of blood oozed from the corner of his mouth, and his face was as white as death. Slowly, like an aged man, he got to his feet. Smeared with dust and blood, he stood stock still, rigid with hatred. Then, with a curse, his face changed to that of a fiend, the tableau broke, and his hand darted towards his shoulder, emerging with a deadly, snub-nosed little Derringer from the concealed holster. His intention was plain: he was going to kill both the horse and its owner. Barclay's finger tightened on the trigger as blind hatred shook his frame.

'Drop it!'

The cold, deadly warning of the words cut into Barclay's demented brain like a knife, and he wheeled to find himself looking straight into the muzzle of Dave Haynes' forty-five. The cowboy had come upon the scene unobserved, leading Grace Tate's horse. Divining the big man's intention, he had slipped behind him. Barclay controlled himself with an effort that cost him dear, for black rage boiled inside him like molten lava.

'Aw,' chided Dave. 'I was hopin' yu'd make a play so I could drop yu.'

Green had turned now, and taken three steps to face the burly rancher.

'Damn yu!' cried Barclay, 'I'll give yu a thousand for the horse, if it's only to shoot it!'

'Yo're a mighty pore loser, Barclay,' was Green's contemptuous comment. 'Get outa my way: I don't want to tread on yu.'

Without another glance at the discomfited Barclay, Sudden turned and swung into the saddle. Barclay cursed as the black stallion received its master's weight without even flickering an ear, and watched the two men as they rode across the wide dusty street to the hotel. Only then did Barclay realise that the brawl had taken place in full view of the hotel, outside which Grace Tate was standing even now.

As they crossed towards the hotel, Dave asked his companion, 'Yu aimin' to commit sooicide, turnin' yore back on a sidewinder like Barclay?'

Green's face was serious. 'Dave, I'm thankin' yu—'

'An' I'm tellin' yu not to,' interrupted his friend. 'Me, I'm sorry I didn't blow out the poison-toad's light anyway.'

'Now that wouldn't have been sensible,' suggested Sudden with a grin.' We already got enough trouble with Her Majesty, without yu go an' exterminate her best friend in these parts.'

'Yu really figger she believes everythin' Barclay told her, Jim?' queried Dave. 'She seems – well – too nice—'

'Ask her yoreself,' Green suggested. 'She shore ain't

gonna be talkin' none to me on the way to the Slash 8.'

He dropped back slightly to allow Dave to present the horse for Grace Tate to mount. He watched his young friend's eager face with keen eyes warmed by friendliness. 'So that's the way she blows, huh? Well, I'm hopin' things'll go yore way, Dave.'

EIGHT

Two days after her arrival at the Slash 8, Grace Tate was finding, to her surprise, that the day-to-day affairs of the ranch interested her, and the very country itself, with its soft pale pink mornings, the cool minty perfume of the sagebrush, and the glorious, multicoloured sunsets were fast making her forget the cities she had left back East. She had to admit – although only to herself: she would never have revealed her feelings – that Green was efficient. He showed her how everything worked, what it cost, why it was being done, in language that was simple enough for her to understand but never gave her the feeling that she was being talked down to. The men obviously liked him; indeed, David – she blushed slightly as she said his name to herself – obviously worshipped the man. Yet she had never heard Green once so much as raise his voice, nor get involved in any kind of argument about how things should be done. The thought that she could not keep her tentative bargain with Barclay had in one way dismayed her, and yet in another, she felt relieved that the decision was out of her hands. Grace Tate was not, however, a girl for long periods of indecision, and thus it happened that the foreman, working down at the corral one morning, turned to find Cookie regarding him thoughtfully.

'The lady boss wants a word with yu, Jim,' he announced.

Sudden found the girl waiting in the big living room.

'I've been looking through my father's papers, Green,' she told Sudden. 'You seem to have taken care of everything that was outstanding.'

'I hope so, ma'am. That's what yore pa asked me to do.'

'I found a letter addressed to me,' she told him. Her voice trembled as she fought for self-control. 'It said ... I should go to see Judge Pringle in South Bend as soon as I could find time. Will you get a horse ready, please?'

To her chagrin, Green displayed not an atom of curiosity regarding her reasons for wanting to visit the Judge. He merely said, 'Yu can't ride there on yore own.' Hoping that he was about to offer to ride as her escort, Grace framed a withering retort, but again Green disappointed her. 'Do yu good to get some fresh air. Dave can ride with you.'

'Very well,' she said. 'I must tell you, Green, that I find this present situation intolerable. I don't like to be in the position of having to ask a complete stranger for every penny that I spend.'

'Shucks, ma'am,' expostulated the foreman, 'Yu can do anythin' yu want. I ain't interferin' in yore personal affairs – it's only ranch business that concerns me. Why – yu needin' somethin'?'

Grace shook her head. Womanlike, she had no particular reason for finding Green's stewardship of the Slash 8 irksome, and in all honesty, admitted to herself that were it not for the conditions of his appointment, she would have been perfectly satisfied to let him run her ranch. As it was, however – she made a frustrated sound.

'I'll get the hoss an' warn Dave,' offered Green, leaving the room. Outside, he allowed a faint grin to cross his face. 'Ain't makin' any progress in the popularity stakes,' he told himself. 'Now I'm the wicked guardian who won't let her buy any pretties, even if she don't want 'em. Huh! – wimmin!'

In short order, a saddled horse was brought to the verandah, and Dave Haynes led the way down to the trail which followed the river towards Thunder Ravine and South Bend. At first, the young cowboy kept a respectable distance from his employer, until Grace, growing tired of the monotony of the plains and her own company, requested him to ride alongside her. After some idle small talk, she asked him about Green.

'He's a fine feller,' was the enthusiastic reply.

'He still looks like a professional gunfighter to me,' Grace said coldly.

'Aw, shucks, ma'am, beggin' yore pardon, but yu wouldn't know a professional gunfighter from a gopher-hole. Don't reckon Jim is a gunman – he ain't got that killer streak. Just the same, I reckon anyone pullin' a gun on him would probably find hisself a mite late.'

He went on to talk to her about some of the famous gunfighters of the times; of Wild Bill Hickok, who had tamed Hays and Abilene, of Wyatt Earp at Dodge City, of Sudden, who had cleaned up Hatchett's Folly; he told her of trail towns and gold towns and the men who had brought law and order into them, armed only with their own courage and their speed on the draw. 'Miss Grace, take my advice an' don't believe anythin' Zack Barclay told yu. He's so crooked that when he dies they're goin' to have to screw him into the ground.'

'He told me that these mysterious Shadows are behind most of the trouble,' Grace persisted. 'Why hasn't anyone tracked them down?'

'Well, there's two answers to that question, ma'am. Yu can take yore pick. First, there's Sheriff Brady's opinion that the Shadows have got a hideout in the hills so well hid that it would take an army to find it; or yu have the other school of thought – to which I subscribe, and so did yore pa and so does Jim – that them *hombres* are what you might call a figment of the imagination.'

'But how can they be?' gasped Grace. 'Surely they have been seen many times? Mr Barclay told me they had robbed the bank at Hanging Rock!'

'That they did,' replied the cowboy, 'an' they're supposed to have done pretty nearly everythin' that's happened around these parts, includin' – beggin' yore pardon, ma'am – ambushin' yore Daddy and Jim Green. But when yu think about her, she don't ring true,' he finished.

Grace's face mirrored her curiosity, and the cowboy went on to explain, ticking off points on his fingers. 'One: how come the Shadows knowed when yore Pa and Green was leavin' town? Two: How come everythin' they've done – apart from robbin' the bank – has been a direct help to Barclay? Three: how can they vanish every time without trace? An' four: why haven't they given Zack Barclay any trouble'

'Oh, come now, David,' interrupted the girl. 'You are making the facts fit the theory, instead of the other way around. Are you seriously suggesting that Barclay is in league with these bandits?'

'Suggestin' he – heck! I'm sayin' it!'

'But that's silly when he has the money to buy whatever he wants without any need to resort to violence.'

'Then answer me this,' asked the cowboy. 'Just what *do* the Shadows want?' Grace fell silent, for indeed, this was a problem to which she had given much thought.

She could not answer Dave's question – indeed, he could not answer it himself. Deep in thought, the two rode in silence through the towering ravine between Thunder Mesa and the river, where the trail narrowed to only a few yards in width. Here, her voice half lost in the swirling noise of the rushing river, Grace spoke again.

'Green told me he was going to sell some cattle in South Bend,' she shouted. 'Surely he can't be thinking of bringing a herd through here?' She gestured at the narrow trail and the towering walls of rock above them.

Dave spoke more reassuringly than he felt.

'Don't yu worry none, ma'am,' he told her. 'Jim knows what he's doin'. If he says he's takin' a herd through to South Bend, he'll take it there, hell or high water.'

Grace Tate did not answer this remark. In fact, she did not speak again until, half an hour later, they were in the main street of the little town of South Bend.

Judge Pringle's house was a small frame building with an ell roof, painted white and green; it lay on the far side of the town just off the road which led, eventually, to Las Cruces.

The judge, whose title was a genuine one and not a courtesy title such as was often found in the West, turned out to be an elderly man of about sixty-five. His tall, stooped frame and pale blue eyes spoke of many hours spent poring over the small print in legal tomes under uncertain light; but his voice was strong, his face rugged and kindly, and his jaw still jutted with determination. His hair was as white as snow.

'So you're George's daughter?' he said, when Grace introduced herself. 'You favour your mother. My, how time flies. The last time I saw you, you had pigtails down to here and freckles all over your face.' He smiled at the recollection. 'I can't tell you how sorry I was to hear of your father's death, my dear. He wrote to me just before . . . it happened, you know.'

'Yes, I know,' Grace told him. 'That's really the reason I am here. My father left me a note saying that I must come and see you.'

'Correct,' the Judge said. 'Why don't you sit down and make yourself comfortable? My housekeeper can bring us some coffee.'

Dave waited until Grace was seated, and then retreated towards the door.

'I'll jest meander down the street, ma'am,' he offered, 'an' come back in about an hour. Yu an' the Judge has got a lot to talk about in private, I'm thinkin'.'

'Oh, David, don't be silly. Judge, this is David Haynes, who works at the Slash 8. Surely there is nothing which he cannot hear – unless Judge, you have any objection?' She raised her eyebrows in a questioning look, and the judge shook his snowy head.

'No, no, my dear,' he told her. 'The situation is relatively simple. Your father sent me what is called in law a power of attorney. That entitles me to handle all his affairs as I see fit, hinging upon two stipulations which your father made. One was that the young man named James Green, in whose abilities your father expressed the greatest confidence, runs all the day-to-day activities of the ranch, and secondly, that you should inherit full title to and control of the Slash 8 upon your twenty-first birthday. Which, I understand, will be in three months' time.'

Grace nodded affirmatively, and the lawyer continued, 'Your father's letter contained information about James Green which I am not at liberty to reveal to you at this time. Suffice it to say that I have made certain inquiries about the young man, and you need have no fear of either his ability or his trustworthiness. I will tell you that one of his references was Governor Bleke of Arizona. The recommendation of a man like Bleke is all the information I need. In view of that, I had no hesitation in allowing Green to continue as foreman of the Slash 8. Had there been any doubt in my mind, or any fear that your father had been hoodwinked, I would have sought an injunction against Green in the Territorial courts. In view of the fact that there is no such doubt, I have executed your father's will in accordance with his wishes.' The old man smiled faintly. 'You must forgive me if I sound like a lawyer, my dear.'

'Thank you, Judge,' said the girl. 'I am correct, then, in saying that I have no power whatsoever at the Slash 8?'

Seeing Grace's downcast expression, the lawyer tried to reassure her.

'My dear, I think you ought to give yourself a chance. You have only been here a short while, and much has happened. Surely, you must realise you could not run the ranch yourself, even if you had control.'

Grace had to admit, albeit reluctantly, that this was true, but she said half-defiantly, 'But then I wouldn't need to. Mr Barclay has already offered to buy the Slash 8 at any fair price I care to name. It seemed to me that selling the ranch would have brought all the troubles in the valley to an end.'

'Obviously neither your father nor Green thought so, Grace,' the old man told her. 'Your father wrote at some length about Mr Barclay.' His tone indicated that none of what her father had written had been complimentary to Barclay, and that Pringle himself seemed to entertain no high opinion of the owner of the Box B. Grace realised that her visit to South Bend had been fruitless, and stood up to leave; Pringle misinterpreted her woebegone expression.

'Please don't be upset,' he said. 'Your first concern is to clear your mortgage with the bank at Hanging Rock. Then you will be financially free, and you can better assess whether you want to sell out or stay. I take it that Green has some plans to raise the money to pay all of your debts?'

'Yes,' said the girl, absently, 'he's going to sell some cattle.'

'Good,' nodded the Judge. 'Let Green run the ranch, my dear. In a few months, if Mr Barclay still wants it and you still feel as you do now, there will be nothing to stop you selling the Slash 8.'

The next morning, as he had previously promised, the owner of the Box B appeared on the trail leading up from the river to the Slash 8. Sudden and Dave were down by the corral finishing mending some bridles, and the young cowboy's eyes narrowed as he identified the approaching rider.

'Zack Barclay!' he spat. 'It shore riles me to see that hydrophoby skunk ridin' up here bold as brass.'

'He's here by Royal invitation – Her Majesty asked him,' Sudden reminded his friend. 'I'm takin' it he ain't favoured the Slash 8 with a visit afore?'

'Never!' snapped Dave, then added, 'an' it ain't no favour, either!'

The owner of the Box B came to a stop in a flurry of dust. To the surprise of both men he came towards them smiling.

'Green,' he began, 'I wanted a word with you.'

'Yu got it,' said Sudden without expression. 'Fire away.'

'I reckon I owe yu an apology for what happened in Hangin' Rock the other day,' Barclay said.

Sudden ignored the extended hand, and anger flushed Barclay's face.

'Yu was about to plug me in the back,' Sudden reminded him, mildly. 'Yu expect to have me forgive and forget it?'

The big rancher kept a tight rein on his temper. There was a lot more at stake than this fool's insulting demeanour – he could be dealt with later. He swallowed his rage, and said, 'I want yu to at least allow me to tell yu I made a mistake.'

'I'm told,' Green said. 'Anything else?'

'Now look here,' Barclay snapped, 'I'm not accustomed to bein' spoken to like this—'

'Then start learnin',' if yu plan to visit the Slash 8,' Dave chimed in coldly. 'Yu're here on sufferance, an' that's all. If it was up to me, I'd run yu off the place on a rail.'

'Why, yu whippersnapper ...' growled Barclay, forgetting his good intentions as a murderous rage flooded his body. He started to dismount, but Sudden's cold voice stopped him in the act.

'Stay there, Barclay,' he ordered. 'Yu ain't had any luck backin' down the Slash 8 so far, an' now wouldn't be a good time to try it again.' He jerked his head slightly to indicate to Barclay that Grace Tate had just stepped on to the verandah of the ranch, having heard their voices from inside.

'Why didn't you tell me Mr Barclay had arrived?' she called.

'I only got here a moment ago, my dear,' Barclay called back, all traces of his rage disappearing from his voice. 'I'll come right up.'

With a final, poisonous glance at the two men by the coral, he walked his horse up to the house.

'Well, I reckon that clears the air some,' Dave breathed.

'Some,' agreed Sudden. 'But I'd still like to know what friend Barclay has on his mind. He shore ain't visitin' the Slash 8 because he likes our purty faces.'

'Wal, if yore purty face was the only reason to come to the Slash 8, I reckon I'd a' left myself by now,' Dave smiled.

'Yeah,' replied Sudden, 'but it ain't *my* purty face yo're interested in, is it?' This shaft was rewarded by a sudden flush around the neighbourhood of his friend's ears, and Dave took a swipe with his hat at his foreman's head. Moving nimbly out of the path of Dave's flailing hand,

Sudden asked plaintively, 'Did I say somethin'?'

'Aw – go climb a tree!' Dave growled, and stamped off about his business.

NINE

From where she sat on the verandah, Grace Tate could see her foreman working by the corral. It was much later, after Barclay had gone, that she realised he was never far away the whole time Barclay was on the ranch. Unobtrusive, out of earshot; but always near. She had divined immediately upon seeing Barclay that he had not been welcomed by Green and David. Barclay, sitting opposite her, sipping a long cold drink which had been served by a scowling Cookie, noticed the frown that crossed Grace's face as the thought struck her, and divining the reason for it, Barclay smiled winningly.

'Yore foreman don't appear to like me,' he told her. 'Well, he has a lesson comin' to him. When I buy the Slash 8, he'll soon learn who's the boss. Meanwhile, don't yu bother yore pretty head about him.'

Grace smiled automatically at the big man's unctuous flattery, and taking this as encouragement, Barclay went on, 'This shore is my lucky day. Not only do I have the pleasure o' seein' yu again, but I think I maybe able to help yu, too.'

'Help me?' asked Grace, in surprise. 'In what way, Mr Barclay?'

'I'd like yu to call me Zack,' he said warmly. 'Well, this conspiracy ...'

Grace Tate's head came up, and a startled expression crossed her face. 'Conspiracy?' she echoed. 'Do you think ...'

'Well, maybe conspiracy is a mite strong,' said Barclay hastily, 'but listen to this: I gave a lot o' thought to what's been happenin' in these parts, an' it struck me that Green could be spearheadin' some kind o' conspiracy to get yore ranch. He rode in here mighty convenient, yu recall?'

Grace nodded, and Barclay went on. 'Only a few hours after his arrival, yore old man – yore father – makes a deal with him about runnin' the ranch. Green suggests that, as yo're under age, he'd better have full control. He's just saved yore pa's life, so naturally, bein' grateful, Tate agrees. In fact, he's bein' hornswoggled. Green arranged the so-called "attack" on the ranch – which no one else except Cookie seen, remember, an' he was tied up – an' then rescues yore pa. Yore pa agrees to give Green control, and sends word to Pringle according. Next thing, yore pa is murdered – an' again our friend Green is Johnny-on-the-spot with no witnesses. An' he has control o' one o' the finest ranches in the Territory. By the time yu come of age, he can milk it dry.'

There was something wickedly logical in the rancher's theory, and despite herself, Grace found the argument swaying her. 'But what about Judge Pringle?' she asked.

'Bah!' snapped Barclay. 'He wouldn't be the first crooked lawyer I've heard of. For all we know, him an' Green are in cahoots.'

Grace shook her head. 'It just doesn't seem possible,' she said faintly. 'Judge Pringle told me Green had the highest references – he had checked up on him.'

'Naturally, he'd say that if they was in cahoots,' Barclay said. 'Did he show yu any o' these references?'

Grace had to admit that he had not.

'There, what'd I tell yu,' Barclay argued. He paused for a moment to let that sink in, and then continued, 'But there's one twist o' the rope our clever friend ain't reckoned on.' Grace looked her question and he said, 'Yes, another way to spoil his game. Look, girl, I'm a rich man, an' goin' to be richer. With yore ranch an' mine combined, we could make an empire outa this valley. Yu'd be a queen, girl, an' yu could have anythin' yu wanted. An' if yu say yes,' he played his trump card, 'yu shore won't be takin' orders from no crooked saddle tramp. What do yu say?'

His hot eyes devoured her greedily, noting the delicate colour under the faint tan on her cheeks, the curling tendrils of hair low on her neck, the long, silken eyelashes. By God, she was a beauty! Apart from giving him the weapon to destroy the banker, she had a proudness which he would enjoy mastering.

'Yu don't have to answer now, girl,' Barclay breathed. 'Just say yu'll think on it. But remember – I'm not a man for waitin'. I want us to be married right away, as soon as yu've decided.'

She nodded, as powerless under his gaze as a sparrow hypnotised by a snake. The clasp of his hand as he rose to leave made her blood burn, but she was thankful that when he spoke it was of something else.

'Don't yu worry none,' he told her. 'I aim to show Mr Green up in his true colours. Remember – the only way to foil him is to marry me.'

Without another word he turned, and mounting his horse, rode out of the environs of the ranch, leaving behind him a young woman puzzled, confused, upset, and strangely impressed – as he had intended that she should be.

It was in this frame of mind that Grace Tate heard from

her foreman later in the day that he intended to drive the herd to South Bend for sale the following day.

'When do you expect to be back?' she asked.

'Thursday, all bein' well,' he said. 'Oughta be a two-day drive, but it won't take all day to get back here.'

'You will bring the money here?'

'Why naturally, ma'am,' said Sudden, surprised by the vehemence of the question. 'I figgered yu'd want to go into town an' see the bank about payin' off yore mortgage. I'll come in with yu, of course.'

'Of course,' Grace said coldly. 'What is the amount of the mortgage?'

'Fifteen hundred dollars, yore pa told me,' Green informed her. 'O' course, there'll probably be some interest charges. I'm hopin' we'll have enough over from the sale o' the herd to pay wages an' buy some feed.'

Grace nodded coolly, and turned on her heel to go into the house. Sudden pushed his sombrero back on his head and rubbed his chin reflectively.

'I'm guessin' friend Barclay's filled her pretty li'l ear with ideas that I'm about to head for tall timber with the money,' he ruminated. 'I shore ain't gettin' nowhere in Her Majesty's good books. It's a wonder she ain't set the Pinkertons on to me.'

That night, over supper, Green outlined his plans for the drive to the assembled men.

'We leave at first light,' he said. 'Gimpy, I want yu on the point.' The grizzled old cowboy nodded, and Dobbs grinned, 'Trust Gimp to get the easy chore,' he said. 'Still, age afore beauty.'

'Don't yu believe that,' Green told him. 'Gimpy's got the toughest spot out of all o' yu. Which is why I'm puttin' him there. We're drivin' across the mountains to South Bend.'

The announcement was greeted with mingled astonishment and disbelief by the Slash 8 riders, and Sudden did not fail to notice that Curt Parr looked particularly crestfallen at this revelation.

'Jim, yu can't be serious,' Dave interjected. 'There ain't no way o' takin' cattle across Thunder Mesa. We'd lose more'n we could afford.'

There was a chorus of agreement, and Curt Parr asked, 'What's wrong with takin' the herd through Thunder Ravine? It ain't easy, o' course, but with care we could get a small herd through an' not too much trouble.'

'Yeah, two at a time an' lose twenty-four hours doin' it,' replied Sudden, 'not to mention bein' sittin' ducks for any Shadows who might happen along.'

'Yu expectin' trouble, then Jim?' Dave asked eagerly.

'My way, no,' Sudden replied. Drawing a piece of paper from his pocket, he demonstrated the route he had planned.

'Yu mean the ol' mine road?' Gimpy asked incredulously. 'Hell, Jim, that's been closed years – there was too much danger from fallin' rocks an' avalanches. All that blastin' years ago loosened the ravine walls when they was huntin' silver up there.'

'Well, I never said it was easy,' Green grinned. 'I just said it was feasible. An' I got my reasons,' he added meaningly.

'How many of us are goin'?' Curt Parr wanted to know.

'Yu, me, Dave, Gimpy, an' Shorty,' replied the foreman. 'Dobbs, I want yu to stay behind with Cookie at the ranch to keep an eye on things. I don't want Miss Tate alone here. *Sabe?*'

Dobbs nodded his understanding, and a reminder that an early start had to be made in the morning ended the discussion and sent the riders back to the bunkhouse hotly debating Sudden's announcement.

Soon after daybreak the drive started. Sudden had already given the men instructions that the cattle were to make their own speed, and Old Mosy, the herd leader, set out at a swinging gait along the trail leading south towards the mountains. Green wanted the herd in good condition for the difficult part of the drive which faced them in the twisting canyons higher up, for he knew that although the route was feasible, there were many dangers on an unknown trail. Nevertheless they made good time; mile after uneventful mile dropped behind them without incident.

A few miles from the opening of the canyon, Gimpy came spurring back from the point. Sudden called a halt for a meal and they broke out the cold food the cook had prepared for them. The cattle milled contentedly, not eager to face the slow uphill climb ahead of them.

'She shore looks unfriendly,' was Gimpy's economic report about the trail ahead. 'Them overhangs look like a good sneeze might drop 'em right on yore head. But like yu said, Jim – she's feasible.'

With this cheering news, they finished their meal and the herd was set in motion once again. Gimpy's report proved accurate.

Sudden, riding at the rear of the herd – 'eatin' dust' as they called it – was beginning to think they would negotiate the uphill part of the canyon without incident when, without warning, two pistol shots rang out. He raced forward to find Curt Parr staring stupidly at the smoking six-gun in his hand.

'What the hell are yu tryin' to do, Parr?' Sudden snapped angrily. 'Bring the whole mountain down on us?'

'I'm plumb sorry, Green,' Parr said earnestly. 'Gun warn't ridin' easy in the holster, an' I pulled her out. Next thing I know, she went off. I can't figger how it happened.'

'Put yore gun in yore saddlebag,' Green told him evenly, 'an' take care it don't happen again, or yu'll wish a mountain *had* fell on yu!'

The foxy cowboy's explanation did not begin to satisfy him, but he had to be content with it. Had Parr some reason for wanting to bring disaster upon the Slash 8 herd? 'More'n likely,' Sudden told himself, and gave the word to push the herd along. He rode within watching distance of Parr, and sure enough, before too long, saw the cowboy dismount. He rode up to where Par was examining his horse's hoof.

'Hoss has gone lame; yu'd better push on without me,' Parr told him. 'I'll catch yu up.'

'Mount up, an' let's see,' was Sudden's reply.

'What's the matter, don't yu believe me?' Parr asked in an aggrieved tone.

'Mount up!' Sudden repeated, 'an' this time keep yore hoss away from these flints.' He pointed to the sharp stones littering the ground. 'When we get back yu can pick up yore time, but right now I need every man I've got, so stay with the herd – an' don't give me any more trouble.'

Presently, the rocky canyon widened, and they were at the pass summit. Before them, the slope stretched gradually downwards through the pine-dotted hills on the south side of the mesa. A natural arena of rock-crowned hills about a quarter of a mile further on made an ideal place for them to bed down the herd for the night, and the Slash 8 men dropped into their blankets, after eating, like dead men.

The next morning they resumed the drive. Spirits were high as they pushed the herd on down the easy, sloping trail. Up ahead, Sudden could hear Gimpy bawling out an unmelodious and bawdy trail song. Apart from one sour look, Parr had had nothing to say to him or anyone else, and they moved forward now without any incident. The frowning canyon was behind them; soon they reached the wide, wagon-wheel-scarred trail leading to South Bend and to the Thunder Mesa mines.

Leaving Gimpy in charge, with an injunction to keep his eye on Parr, Sudden rode on ahead of the oncoming herd. He found Pat Newman in a small, but neat office near the mine-shaft on the hillside. Newman's eyes widened when he saw his visitor.

'Come to tell me the deal's off?' he asked Sudden.

'Nope. Come to tell yu to look out o' the window,' was the smiling reply. Newman crossed quickly to the window which looked out along the trail; not far away he could see the dusty cloud raised by the Slash 8 herd. He turned to Sudden with his hand outstretched.

'Yu win your bet,' he said. 'Let's go and watch them being loaded into the pens.'

The two men walked out to the corrals and they watched while the herd was corralled and counted. When the hot dusty work was finished, Newman invited Sudden back to the office, having detailed a couple of miners to see that the Slash 8 crew was fed and given something to drink. Before they trooped off, Sudden drew Dave Haynes to one side.

'Tell the others to head back for the Slash 8 when they're through eatin', an' spread the word I'm goin' back through Thunder Ravine.'

Dave's expression betrayed his burning curiosity at these orders, but Sudden gave him no time to frame a question. The Slash 8 foreman turned on his heel an joined Newman in the office, where the two men were brought a good meal by a resident mine cook.

'Yu shore do yoreselves proud up here,' Sudden remarked. 'That's near as good cookin' as we get on the Slash 8.'

'If yu get better food than this, I'm anglin' for an invitation right now,' smiled Newman.

'Yu got it,' Sudden told him.

The dishes were pushed to one side, and the two men settled down to business. Newman totalled some figures on a sheet of paper and showed the final amount to his guest.

'You agree the figure, Mr Green?'

'Looks fine to me, seh,' Sudden told him. 'Five hundred head at five dollars a head: that's twenty-five hundred dollars.'

'You don't seem interested in whether I'm cheating you,' Newman pointed out. 'You haven't asked me what I was paying Marty Black.'

'Shucks,' smiled Sudden. 'If yu was cheatin' me, I'd find out. An' I'd probably get a little impatient with yu.'

Newman surveyed the two guns strapped low on his guest's' hips.

'I thought that,' he murmured. 'You're getting the same price Black gets.'

'Never imagined it would be anything else,' Sudden said.

'What I can't understand is how you got the herd through the mountains in such prime condition,' Newman posed

'She was a good deal easier than I'd hoped,' Sudden admitted. 'If yo're interested, I'm guessin' we could make a regular deal on this.'

'We'll talk about it,' Newman said. 'If you can deliver in this condition and give me a good price, I'll continue to buy your beef.'

The two men shook hands on their bargain, and Newman counted out payment for the herd from a safe. Sudden was expressing his thanks when Dave returned to say that the crew was about to start back.

'Yu serious about ridin' back through Thunder Ravine?' Dave asked, and when Sudden nodded, the cowboy cried, 'Yo're off yore rocker, ridin' that road with all this dinero in yore pocket.' He gestured at the stack of notes on the table.

'I ain't,' grinned Sudden, and when Dave looked his puzzlement, explained, 'Yo're takin' the money, an' yo're goin' back with the others. By the way, what time did Parr leave?'

'How d'you know that?' Dave asked in surprise. 'Well, never mind, yo're right. He slid out about twenty minnits back. Said he warn't hungry.'

'I'll bet,' said Sudden, non-committally. 'Here – take good care o' this, it's about ten years wages to ordinary folks like yu an' me.'

Dave looked at the thick roll of bills as if they might suddenly bite him, then stowed them hastily into a pocket.

'Yo're takin' a long chance on me, come to that,' he said soberly.

'What – yu rob Her Majesty? That'll be the day,' the foreman told him. 'Hit the trail, little man, an' don't stop to pick no daisies.'

Newman smiled at the exchange between the two men.

'You mind telling me what that was all about?' he asked Sudden.

'Well, seh,' the Slash 8 man replied, 'them Shadow *hombres* have been havin' all the fun up to now. I just figger it's about time the Slash 8 joined the dance.'

TEN

Arriving in South Bend, Sudden pursued the impulse he had had on the trail to visit Judge Pringle. The Judge received him in his 'office', a small, book-cluttered room.

'I am glad you decided to come and see me, Mr Green,' the Judge began. 'You know, of course, that George Tate wrote to me about you?'

Sudden nodded. 'I figgered he might, seh. Did he tell yu the whole tale?'

When Pringle indicated that Tate had kept the cowboy's secret, Sudden smiled. 'That's about the way he was, seh. But I'd better tell yu anyway.' And the old lawyer listened spellbound as the tall young visitor told him the story of how he had come to be known as 'Sudden', the outlaw.

When he had finished, Sudden's face was grim, but Pringle reassured him immediately. 'I am glad you told me, Jim. It doesn't alter anything, of course. I begin to realise what George meant when he wrote that I must judge you on your actions thus far, and nothing else. He also told me to be prepared for a surprise, and I am surprised. One does not expect a hunted outlaw to be backed by a character reference from the Governor of Arizona.'

'I once did him a favour,' was Green's only comment,

and the lawyer asked no more.

'Is there anything else I can do?' asked Pringle.

'A couple o' things, Judge. Yu got the time and the contacts; I don't. First of all, do you know what the Slash 8 mortgage is?'

'I'm almost sure it's fifteen hundred dollars. George wrote me about it. He was short of ready cash to make improvements so he negotiated the loan at Hanging Rock, using the ranch as security.'

'Yu got a copy o' the actual mortgage, Judge?'

'No,' replied the old man, 'but I can easily get one. Do you want me to?'

They talked for a while longer, and the Judge promised to look into several matters for which Green could simply not spare the time.

'Rely on me,' Pringle told the Slash 8 man. 'I'll do everything I can.' The two men shook hands and parted, and Green mounted up and rode out on to the deserted trail.

He was not hurrying; he did not want to reach the gloomy Thunder Ravine before full darkness fell, and so he allowed Thunder to pick his own way and his own speed. Dark indeed it was inside the inky confines of the ravine. To his left he could hear the hiss and tumble of the Sweetwater as it rushed across the canyon's jagged floor. Thunder stepped daintily along the narrow trail, the sound of his hoofs echoing from the dripping canyon walls. Without warning, a voice broke into Sudden's apparent reverie, and he looked up to see two shadowy figures blocking the trail ahead of him.

'Stick 'em up, pronto!' came the barked order.

The Slash 8 man could just about discern in the darkness the shape of the two men, their faces concealed behind bandannas, pistols in their hands with the muzzles unwaveringly trained upon him. Sudden raised his hands and, at another command, kicked his feet free from the stirrups and slid down to the ground. The two men stepped apart, covering him from both sides; their figures became more distinct as they came closer

'All right, Green, hand it over!'

'Hand what over?' asked Sudden innocently.

'Don't play dumb,' snapped the masked man on the right who was doing all the talking. 'Hand over the dough yu got for sellin' yore herd!'

Sudden laughed aloud, a sound which caused the two hold-up men to flinch slightly, and eye their prisoner warily. 'I ain't got the money,' Sudden told his inquisitor. 'I sent it back with one o' the men.'

'A likely yarn,' snapped Talker. 'Frisk him, Ray!'

The man on the left gritted an oath at his companion. 'Ain't yu got more sense?' he snarled.

'Get on with it,' ordered Talker. 'What diff'rence does it make, anyway?'

'None at all,' agreed Sudden. 'Pleased to meetcha again, Ray. How's yore head?'

The man Ray did not answer, but with a muttered imprecation, sheathed his gun and made a rapid, but thorough search of the prisoner. Finding nothing, he went quickly over the horse: saddle bags, poncho, everywhere money might have been hidden. There was nothing and he told his companion so.

'I done told yu that already,' Sudden said reasonably. 'I guess yu just been told so many lies in yore life yu wouldn't know the truth if it walked up an' kicked yu.'

Ray growled beneath his mask, and with an angry gesture turned and thrust his revolver into Sudden's face.

'Shut yore yap!' he threatened. 'I owe yu already – it won't take much to talk me into blowin' out yore light!'

His movement was a mistake. With a lightning move, Sudden flung his left arm forward and across, knocking

Ray's gun muzzle wide of his body. At the same moment, his right hand came up in a short, jolting arc that caught the bandit flush on the jaw. Under the weight of this wicked punch the recipient was hurled backwards, blundering into his companion, whose hastily fired shot at the Slash 8 man went wide and whined off the canyon wall. Sudden's hand flashed towards his own guns and he drove a bullet into the dark mass of the outlaw's body before the man could pull the trigger again. The man folded down into the darkness of the canyon floor as Sudden turned, and was into the saddle and pounding away to safety before the reeling Ray could realise what had happened.

Sudden pushed his horse hard from then on, and reached the ranch, without further incident. Dave met him at the corral where he had been waiting anxiously for his friend's return.

'I figgered somethin' o' the sort was likely,' Sudden told him after describing the events in the canyon. 'I was pretty shore that word would have been passed to the Shadows that we was makin' our drive. I imagine they holed up for us at Thunder Ravine: They musta got a nasty shock when we didn't turn up.'

'Yeah, but how did they know yu'd be comin' back that way?' Dave put in, puzzled.

'I told them,' Sudden smiled. Dave's blank expression made him laugh, and he explained. 'Remember I told yu to spread the word among the boys about me comin' back that way?'

'Yu mean – one of us passed the word to the Shadows?'

'That I do,' said Sudden, his tone turned grim. 'Let's go talk to him.'

With these words, the foreman headed with long strides towards the bunkhouse, where lights in the windows indicated that the Slash 8 crew was not yet abed. There was a chorus of greeting as Sudden entered the long room, but it died quickly as those present saw the expression on their foreman's face. Sudden wasted no time; he confronted Parr, whose shifty eyes failed to meet the icy gaze boring into him.

'What become o' yu at the mine, Parr?' asked Sudden softly.

'I left early,' was the sullen reply. 'Figgered my hoss might go lame again – which it did. The boys got home afore me, in the end.'

'Not surprisin',' was the cold comment. 'Yu took the long way home.' Green looked at Parr levelly. 'I told yu on the drive yu was through, an' that goes. Now I'm tossin' in somethin' extra. Get off the Slash 8 an' don't come back.'

'Yu'll regret this, Green,' spat Parr, meeting Sudden's gaze defiantly.

'I doubt it,' was the reply. 'I ain't never regretted riddin' myself o' liars an' cowards,' and then, as Parr made an abortive move towards his gun, he snapped, 'Don't go near that unless yu want to stay here – permanent.'

For a few seconds, the two men faced each other; there was an astonished silence in the bunkhouse as the rest of the crew watched the half-crouched figure in the centre of the room. Then Parr's gaze flickered away from the foreman's.

'Like I said – yeller,' sneered Sudden, half turning as if to walk away.

'Damn yu, Green!' screeched Parr, 'I'll—'

He did not finish the threat, if such it was to have been. Before his clutching hand could curl around the butt of his six-gun, Sudden had whirled like a panther. His left hand clamped upon the other's right wrist like a band of steel, while his right seized Parr's throat. He shook the man the way a terrier shakes a rat, back and forth, sinking his steely grip deeper into Parr's neck. The other, his face purpling, eyes bulging as Sudden's grip cut off his wind, was near suffocation when, with a contemptuous thrust, the foreman flung Parr headlong upon the floor. The cowboy lay there, wheezing and gasping, his tortured lungs labouring for oxygen. It was some moments before he could stagger to his feet, by which time Green had counted out some money from the roll which Dave had handed to him in the corral. He tossed the money at Parr's feet.

'There's a month's pay,' he snapped, 'which is forty dollars more'n yo're worth. Get yore gear an' punch the breeze.'

With an evil look, Parr collected his scant belongings and slouched out, with Sudden behind him, ready for any further show of resistance. But the man was beaten; he saddled his horse and disappeared into the darkness without another word.

ELEVEN

The next morning, Sudden announced to the Slash 8 crew that he was planning on doing what he called 'a little pokin' around', and without further elaboration he saddled his black horse, packed a bedroll and some food, filled a canteen of water, and set out alone towards the river trail. He had not gone very far, however, when the thunder of hoofs behind him caused him to stop and await the arrival of a defiant-looking Dave who pulled alongside him and, with a grin, pointed out that he was coming along.

'Shucks, no tellin' what might happen to yu alone,' he told his foreman. 'I figgered yu'd need a wet-nurse, an' I done elected myself.'

Sudden argued with his young friend for a few moments, but truth to tell, found himself not sorry to have company. He explained his feelings to Dave as they rode together along the banks of the Sweetwater.

In due course the two men reached the point on the river where the burbling little stream, which Dave had once told Sudden was called the Bonito, joined the larger river. Just above this confluence was a well-marked ford across the river, and the two men splashed across it and up the far bank. Here, a roughly painted notice board met their gaze.

BOX B Land
Stay Off
This means You.

'Friendly cusses, ain't they?' remarked Sudden.

'Very. An' they mean it. Couple o' *hombres* that thought they didn't wound up pickin' lead out o' their anatomies.'

'Don't yu fret, little man – we ain't pickin' no Box B daisies. Our trail lies over yonder.' He gestured towards the left, where a shifting shimmer of bright heat played across the horizon.

'The Badlands!' Dave exclaimed. 'Yu aimin' to go in there?'

'Shore as yo're slow on the uptake,' grinned Sudden. 'Of course, if she sounds too much like hard work, yu can allus roll yore tail back home.'

Dave shook his head grimly. 'Nope. I reckon if you're fool enough to ride in there, the least I can do is come with yu to make shore yu don't break yore toe or somethin'.'

The two riders moved on, skirting the trail which would have led them down to the Barclay place, and in a short while were in the barren sandy wastes of the Badlands. Here, Nature changed her face, and it did not seem possible that this savage landscape could exist so close to the pleasant rolling range that they had so recently crossed.

The midday sun was now growing unbearable, and Dave heaved a genuine sigh of relief as his companion called a halt. Together, the two men sought the shelter of a rocky gully where overhanging shelves of rock threw a welcome shade. Here, they watered the horses thriftily and with a small fire of tinder-dry wood, made coffee and ate some of the food Green had brought.

'Didn't yu bring anything with yu to eat?' asked Sudden in mock exasperation.

'Hell, I didn't know we was goin' picknickin',' admitted Dave. 'If I'd'a known I'd've brought some o' those fish eggs . . . what d'yu call 'em—'

'Caviare, yu mean?' asked Sudden.

'That's the one,' enthused Dave. 'An' some o' them other fancy foods they eat back East.'

'Shucks, yu wouldn't like 'em,' Sudden told him. 'I tried that fancy eatin' one time. Shore pretty to look at, but they don't do more than whet a man's appetite. I'd sooner have bacon an' beans out in the open than all yore fancy city meals.'

They finished their meal, cleaned out the plates with sand, put out their fire by pouring the coffee grounds upon it and kicking sand upon the hissing embers. Within half an hour, they were back in the saddle heading westwards.

Eventually Dave felt constrained to break the silence once more, and inquired of his companion their destination.

'Up ahead a ways,' was the reply, which gave the young cowboy no information at all. 'Bloomin' clam,' he muttered, 'I could get more chatter outa one o' them cactus trees.' A covert glance revealed that if the other had heard this remark he was not going to be drawn into comment. With a shrug, Dave settled grimly into his saddle, hunching his shoulders against the blasting heat and trying to ignore the itching trickle of sweat beneath his clothes. The two men moved on into the faceless desert.

Curt Parr was in an evil mood. After his summary

dismissal from the Slash 8, he had ridden into Hanging Rock. There he had discovered that his grievances only floated on top of the liquor he poured down his throat. The fiery spirit did, however, inflate his shattered conceit, and by the time he had consumed almost a bottle of Diego's *tequila* he could see very clearly how indispensable he was to Zachary Barclay. His fuddled brain reasoned that since the Box B owner had been responsible for his working on the Slash 8 – and the others before it – it was now Barclay's responsibility – no, duty – to grubstake him before he departed this part of the country. 'I got plenty on yu, Zack ol' boy,' he mumbled. 'Yu better be – reasonable.'

It was dawn by the time he reached the Box B, but the slow, solemn beauty of the sunrise meant less than nothing to Parr. At this early hour, he encountered no one until he was in the yard of the Box B, where a light shining from the main house window apprised him of the fact that someone was already up and about. Congratulating himself on his luck, Parr stumbled up the steps and hammered on the door. In a moment it was thrown open, and Parr's drunken warmth froze in his veins as the barrel of a .45, held in the huge fist of Burley Linkham, was thrust into his face.

'It's me, Link, Curt Parr,' he gasped hurriedly. Linkham's face did not change, nor did he lower the six-gun. He simply looked at the snivelling Parr, whose liquor bolstered courage was rapidly evaporating. 'Burley, for Godsake, it's me, Curt. I got to see Barclay,' he whimpered.

'What for?' was the cold query.

Without volition, Parr's voice spilled out of him; he recounted the events of the proceeding evening at the Slash 8, his dismissal, his need of a grubstake. Linkham cut in on his whining, harshly. 'What makes yu think anyone cares about yore bad luck?' he growled callously.

Parr drew himself up carefully. 'Link,' he said, in as level a voice as he could muster, 'Just 'cause I allus reported to yu, don't mean yo're the boss. I want to talk to Zack.'

'What about, Curt?' Linkham's voice had gone softer, soothing. Parr felt better. Linkham knew that he was important. That Zack needed him.

'Yu know,' he told Linkham coldly. 'I need a stake. I'm gettin' out.'

'Well, OK, yo're goin'. Why should Zack stake yu?'

'Because I know plenty, that's why.' Parr's defiance was his last effort. He stood there, hating this big brutal man who stood between him and Barclay. Linkham would show no sympathy, offer to help. Only Barclay. Barclay would have to listen.

'What do yu know, Curt?' Linkham's voice was almost gentle.

'Enough,' snapped Parr. 'Now let me talk to Zack.'

Linkham's answer was a casual, almost lazy movement with his right hand. It described a sort, vicious arc, and the six-gun it held caught Part across the bridge of the nose and hurled him backwards off the porch, writhing in agony and pawing at the blood spurting from his shattered face. Linkham looked at him unemotionally.

'Yu know nothin',' he told the prostrate figure in the dust. 'Yu'll say nothin'. If yo're in this country tomorrow I'll kill yu.'

Linkham stepped back quietly into the house. The whole scene had taken only a few minutes; moving carefully, he opened the door of Barclay's bedroom and listened. The sound of even breathing told him Barclay was not yet awake. He nodded to himself, and said, 'What he don't know won't bother him.' An evil smile lit his face as he returned to the window and watched the blood-spattered Curt Parr climb into the saddle and ride off into the morning, his body lurching with every movement that the animal made.

TWELVE

The trail across the Badlands was at best only faintly defined, and several times, Dave found himself lost in admiration of his foreman's uncanny skill in charting their way across the sandy waste; he relieved himself of a long-drawn sigh as a small clump of trees appeared on the rim of the desert, and Green, hearing the sound, straightened up in the saddle and grinned, 'Water ahead. Yu can have a bath – an' yu could use one.'

'Shucks,' replied Dave. 'I just hope I get to the water afore yu dip yore beak in, or she'll be plumb spoiled for drinkin'.'

With a whoop of high spirits which came as a complete surprise to Dave, Sudden whisked off his hat and slapped Dave's horse across the ears. The young cowboy spent the next few minutes trying to control his pony, which was giving a creditable imitation of a horse trying to fly; by the time he had the animal under control once more, the Slash 8 foreman was a fast-receding figure at the head of a plume of dust arrowing towards the waterhole some miles ahead. With a mild oath, Dave pointed his still-edgy bronc after Green, and rocketed in pursuit.

'Shore beats all the way that gent'll look so sleepy, an' then jus' when yo're lulled, he'll pull a fool stunt like that,' he soliloquised.

By the time he reached the waterhole, Green was already hunkered in the shade of one of the few trees, starting a fire. His horse, unsaddled, was cropping the sandy tufts of grass

'What kept yu?' Green asked innocently as Dave reined up alongside. 'No – don't tell me. The minnit I leave yu alone for a second, yu go an' get yoreself lost. Shore beats me how yu ever find yore way home, the way yu keep harin' all over the landscape. O' course, if yu could control that bone-bag yu call a hoss....'

He subsided into laughter as Dave's pent-up fury threatened to burst him at the seams, and continued to smile as his companion's choicest invective rolled like a cascade about his ears. When Dave began to run out of adjectives and breath, Green inquired, 'Yu want some coffee? I figgered so. In which case, whyn't yu just toddle down to the water an' fill thisyere pot. And wash out yore mouth while yo're at it . . . I ain't never heard such scandalous talk.'

With a mock swipe at Sudden's head, Dave took the coffee pot and proceeded down to the edge of the pool where its muddy sides were pocked by the footprints of the many animals that drank there. He caught a glimpse of the track of a mountain cat, and turned to call Green.

He never heard the shot. Parr, up on the hillside overlooking their camp, had been watching the two men ever since they arrived at the waterhole. When Haynes finally took the coffee pot down to the water's edge, the darkvisaged ambusher had his first clear aim at the two men, and he acted almost instantly. His first shot dropped Dave Haynes like a log half in, half out of the water, and he whipped the Winchester around like a snake as Green leaped to his feet, moving with a powerful thrusting leap towards his saddle and the rifle in his scabbard on it. Parr's second shot knocked the Slash 8 foreman sidewards and back into the shadow of the tree, where he lay unmoving, curiously huddled, with one arm outstretched and the other doubled beneath his body.

Parr let five minutes go by. Then another five.

Neither man moved. Haynes lay as he had fallen, and from his vantage point, Curt Parr could see the slow stain of red darkening the water. Green lay in black shadow but there was no hint of movement from his body. Parr twitched the bush behind which he lay; nothing happened. Gingerly, he raised his Stetson on the barrel of the rifle, above the level of the bush.

'Cashed, the pair of 'em,' he exulted. 'So much for yu, Mr Smart-Aleck Green. Yore sidekick's hard luck: he picked the wrong day to ride with yu.' When he was below the level of the ridge, he levered a fresh round into the chamber of the Winchester. Then, leading his horse, he carefully approached the camp-site. Ahead of him, Haynes lay where he had fallen. Parr approached the slumped form of the Slash 8 rider cautiously, his rifle at the ready. Haynes did not move, and the pool of blood in which he lay made it obvious to the bushwhacker that Haynes would give him no trouble. Skirting the water's edge, he sidled over to where Green lay, face down. Leaving the horse's reins trailing, he poked his foot under Green's ribs to turn the body over. As he did so, Sudden exploded into activity. His hand grabbed Parr's foot and jerked it upwards, throwing the ambusher over and back. Parr's rifle went off but the slug whined harmlessly into the air. He hit the ground with a bone-shaking thud, the rifle jarred from his grasp. Above him, eyes slitted menacingly, Sudden stood straddle-legged, the bore of his .45 poised like a rock three inches from Parr's face. The ambusher recoiled in horror, crying 'Don't shoot me!'

'I shore oughta,' grated Green savagely. 'I oughta blow out yore light – an' it would pleasure me to do it – but I got a hunch yo're goin' to be useful, so I'm lettin' yu go on livin' *for the moment.*' There was no mistaking his meaning, and Parr nodded vehemently, offering no protest as Green quickly and efficiently lashed Parr's hands behind him, rolled the man on his face, and then tied the bound hands to Parr's ankles, so that the bushwhacker was bent backwards like a drawn bow.

'Now I aim to see whether Dave is alive or dead,' Green told him. 'Yu'd better pray he's still breathin'.'

Without another glance at the abject form of his would-be assassin, Green crossed quickly to where Dave lay. A hasty examination reassured him. Parr's bullet had hit Dave high on the shoulder blade, and torn its way out near the collarbone. The young Slash 8 rider was going to be weak from loss of blood, but it looked much worse than it was. Sudden breathed a sigh of relief and set to work to clean the wound and bandage it with strips torn from Dave's shirt.

Half an hour later the young man was conscious, propped up against the tree and regarding his partner with puzzled eyes.

'Hell,' he said weakly. 'It can't be Heaven – they wouldn't allow such ornery-lookin' angels on the place.' Then his eyes fell upon Parr, still lying trussed where the foreman had roughly thrown him. 'What's Parr doin' here?' And when Green had told him, 'That – sidewinder! Whyfor'd he bushwhack us, Jim?'

'He ain't said,' Green informed him, adding meanfully, 'yet.' Parr paled as the Slash 8 duo glared at him malignantly. His coward's brain was busy with wild plans for escape but he knew in his heart that he did not have the courage to try and make a break for it. He had seen that cold-eyed devil in action, and he knew that, unless Green were dead, he would not escape. Almost as if reading his mind, the subject of Parr's thoughts came over and stood looking down at him.

'If yo're thinkin' of escapin', forget it. Yo're on borrowed time right now. Yu an' me is goin' to have a little chat. I'm goin' to ask yu some interestin' questions, an' yo're goin' to give me some interestin' answers.' When Parr's expression turned to a sneer, Sudden grinned, and turning to Dave, he said, 'By the way, did I ever tell yu I was brung up by Injuns?'

The wounded man shook his head, puzzled at this change of tack in the conversation. 'No, can't say yu ever did, Jim,' he replied.

He had not the remotest idea what Green was leading up to, but he was well aware that Green rarely waggled his chin just for the exercise, so he kept his silence as Green went on, almost dreamily.

'One o' the things they did teach a man real good was how to make prisoners talk. They was real experts. I never seen a man that could last fifteen minutes. They either talked fast, or they never talked no more.'

Catching Sudden's intent, Dave played up to it. He saw Parr's eyes roll white in the approaching dusk, and asked a question.

'They ever teach yu any o' the tricks to make a man talk, Jim?'

An almost imperceptible nod and grin showed that Green had appreciated Dave's quickness of wit in divining his intention.

'Shore,' he said. 'I was just thinkin', maybe I oughta practice up a mite. Parr here knows a few things we need to know. Maybe he'll tell us about them without any persuasion, though.'

Parr spat an obscenity.

'One o' the tough ones,' Green smiled coldly. 'They sometimes last about three minutes longer.' He ostentatiously withdrew a Bowie knife from his saddle bags and thrust the long blade into the glowing embers of the fire that he had built when tending Dave's wounds. He then went into the brush and rummaged around there for a few moments, returning with a stout branch four feet in length, which he proceeded to strip of its branches. This, he also thrust into the coals. Parr watched this performance with eyes which had suddenly become fear-widened and white-rimmed.

'I better warn yu – this ain't pretty,' he warned Dave.

'Good!' enthused that worthy. 'I'm hopin' Parr's got more guts than I think he has, so yu can give him a real workin' over. I'm a-goin' to *enjoy* this!'

Green nodded, then walked over to Parr, whose bonds he then deliberately and methodically tested. Nodding once more, he turned away from the prisoner and withdrew the now red-hot knife from the fire. Hefting it carefully, he turned back to the prone man, who uttered a moaning scream and tried ineffectually to wriggle away from his tormentor. Green's face was hard and unrelenting.

'Parr,' he intoned, 'I want some information an' I want it fast!' he waved the glowing blade of the knife in front of Parr's sweating face.

'Yu – yu can't!' Parr gasped. 'Yu wouldn't . . . yo're a white man. Yu wouldn't pull an Injun trick like that....'

'I could an' I will,' Green said grimly, 'unless yore jaw loosens some. First question: who's yore boss?'

Parr hesitated. Then, incredibly, he shook his head. Fear of Sudden was one thing; fear of Barclay and Linkham was another. He did not really believe that Green would use Indian torture on him.

'Yo're a fool!' snapped Sudden, 'an' I got no time for fools.' He bent and ripped away the front of Parr's shirt. Holding Parr's shoulder in a grip like steel, he brought the glowing knife blade inexorably closer to the shrinking skin.

'Barclay! Barclay hired me! Damn yu, put that thing away!' the bound man screeched.

'Barclay hired yu personal?' Sudden insisted.

'No, not personal. Linkham did all the hirin', but he's Barclay's foreman. It's the same thing.'

'Yu reported to Linkham, then, not Barclay?'

'Yes, yes, I told yu, yes! Put that damned knife down....'

'Right, full marks so far. Now the big question, Parr: who ramrods the Shadows?' He brought the knife back in front of Parr's eyes. 'Talk, damn yu!'

'Linkham! Linkham runs the Shadows.'

'Yo're shore?'

Parr nodded vehemently. 'There's eight of them: Morley, Smith, Callaghan, Roberts, MacAlmon, a fellow called Ray, an' Bull Pardoe. He's in charge when Linkham ain't there, which is most o' the time.'

'Is he the big broken-nosed feller?'

Parr nodded, eager to please now, his resistance gone completely.

'Bull don't give no orders, though. They only do what Link tells them. The rest of the time they hole up.'

'Where?'

'There's a canyon – I could take yu there,' Parr said. A fleeting expression of cunning momentarily lighting his foxy eyes.

'Yu ain't goin' anyplace, Parr,' Sudden told him coldly, 'so don't strain yore tiny little brain. Yu just tell me where they hole up – an' don't lie to me. I'd take exception to it.' He gestured with the knife again.

'A canyon, I told yu,' Parr blurted hastily. 'I'm tellin' yu the truth. Yu head up northwest through the Badlands along the bases o' these hills until yu come to a canyon. Yu'll know it 'cause they's some rocks that look like a lizard. The canyon looks like a blind draw, but it opens into a little valley. There's a shack there. That's where they hole up.'

Green looked dubious. He regarded the prisoner for a moment, and then said, 'Parr, I think yo're lyin'—'

'No!' screeched Parr, 'I ain't! Yu got to believe me!'

Sudden smiled to himself. Then, nodding as if coming to a decision, he faced the prisoner.

'I'll take a look.' He turned back to Dave. 'Can yu get back to the Slash 8 on yore own?'

Dave's face turned sullen. 'Hell, Jim, I'm OK,' he said. 'Let me come with yu.'

'No, Dave. If yu can get back to the ranch, I want yu there. I'm goin' to mosey up an' take a look for this shack. If I ain't back inside o' forty-eight hours, get over to Judge Pringle at South Bend an' tell him what happened. He'll know what to do. Now don't argue with me, Dave. I got a feelin' yo're goin' to be needed at the ranch, an' yu got to get that shoulder looked after.'

Dave grumbled mightily, but he knew in his heart that Green was right; in this condition, he would be a hindrance to the foreman.

Sudden turned now to Parr. 'I'm turnin' yu loose, Parr,' he told the wide-eyed prisoner. 'I'd guess from the look o' yore face that yore old bosses have given yu marchin' orders. I'm reinforcin' whatever they told yu. Get outa this country, pronto. If I hear o' yore bein' seen around here, I'll take after yu personally.' He bent and whispered something to Parr, who recoiled and looked at him in amazement.

'Yo're—'

'Yes, I am!' Sudden interrupted, 'so yu know I ain't just talkin'.' He slashed the man's bonds, and pulled him roughly to his feet. 'Git!' he told the battered Parr. Stumbling, uncertain, terrified, the bandit mounted his horse and disappeared into the darkness.

'Yu reckon that was wise, Jim?' Dave asked. 'He might go straight to warn them yo're comin'.'

'No,' Sudden told him. 'Parr is finished, an' he knows it. He ain't worth the price of a bullet. Let him go – we got bigger fish to fry.'

THIRTEEN

It took Dave four hours' straight riding to reach the Slash 8, and his hail was answered at the ranch house by Gimpy and Grace Tate, who appeared on the porch. Swaying slightly in the saddle, dust-caked, his shirt in tatters and the blood seeping slowly from his opened wound, Dave looked like the survivor of a massacre.

The others came tumbling out of the bunkhouse, and tender hands helped Dave down from the saddle. He was taken into the house, where Grace Tate, dismissing his protests with a wave of the hand, took care of his wounded shoulder, exclaiming softly, while Dave related the events of the day in terse, rapid sentences. When he came to the events of Parr's perfidious ambush, threatening sounds came from one or two of the Slash 8 men, and Shorty exclaimed, 'Why, the dirty...!'

Dave found himself unable to ignore the cool touch of Grace Tate's hands as she efficiently dressed his aching shoulder. To occupy his thoughts, he asked those assembled whether anything had happened during his and Green's absence.

Gimpy nodded grimly, and receiving Grace's permission to tell the story with a nod from her, he told Dave that he had ridden into Hanging Rock with Grace that morning to pay off their mortgage. When they had arrived at the bank, de Witt had received them with some courtesy, and had insisted upon Sheriff Brady's being present before he would discuss the mortgage on the Slash 8 with them.

'What on earth would Brady need to be there for?'

In sentences no less terse than those Dave had himself used, Gimpy told him of the events which had transpired in de Witt's office. Brady had huffed in and taken his place beside the banker. Grace laid the money on the banker's desk and asked him to count it. He did so, and then looked at her with raised eyebrows.

'There are only fifteen hundred dollars here, Miss Tate,' he said, surprise in his voice.

Grace was nonplussed by his statement, and said as much. 'I was under the impression that fifteen hundred dollars was the amount involved, Mr de Witt.'

'Then you have been misinformed, madam. That is the reason that I asked Sheriff Brady to come along.' He delved into a drawer of his desk and produced a piece of paper. It was note-paper of the Hanging Rock Bank, and was in the form of a loan agreement between George Tate and the Bank. 'You will see that the amount involved is, in fact, four thousand five hundred dollars,' the banker told them coolly. 'Surely you knew that?'

'No, I did not, and I do not,' Grace said, equally coldly. 'I am sure there is some mistake, Mr de Witt.'

'That is your father's signature, is it not, Miss Tate?' asked de Witt. Grace nodded dumbly, and he continued, 'Surely you must have known that the amount was larger than fifteen hundred dollars? You must have realised that I should hardly have called your mortgage for so small an amount?'

Stricken to silence by this revelation, Grace had simply stood there while the banker told her that, while he had been fully prepared to wait until she had sold her cattle to realise the money to pay off her mortgage, she would appreciate that he could no longer wait.

'I am afraid that I shall have to foreclose on your mortgage,' deWitt said with finality, 'unless you can raise the other three thousand dollars inside the original deadline. I am a man of honour, Miss Tate. I offered your man Green ten days. That concession still has forty-eight hours to run. I give you until then to raise the money. Failing that, I will ask Sheriff Brady to foreclose immediately upon the Slash 8, and sell the ranch in public auction. Sheriff?'

Brady had stepped forward, pompous and self-important.

'Forty-eight hours,' he snapped. 'Then the Slash 8 goes up for sale.'

Gimpy and the mistress of the Slash 8 had left town like thieves, they both knew that there was not the slightest hope of their being able to raise three thousand dollars within the deadline so callously set by the banker.

'So there we are,' Gimpy said. 'Yu ain't the on'y one been havin' fun.'

'Brady can't sell off the ranch,' Dave said. 'It ain't legal!'

'That's the worst part of it, Dave,' Grace told him sadly. 'It is legal. Every bit of it entirely legal and we cannot oppose it. I shall have to sell the ranch to Mr Barclay.'

'Yu can't do that!'

'David, I must. Barclay would at least pay what the ranch is worth. If I wait until the mortgage is foreclosed, I'll lose everything.'

'That's what I can't figger,' Dave mused. 'Why should Barclay pay yu full price for the ranch when, if he waits forty-eight hours, he can get it for a song?'

Grace flushed, then, chin high, admitted, 'There was ... a condition. Zachary Barclay asked me to marry him.'

Dave stood up, shaking off the hands which tried to restrain him.

'Marry that skunk? Yu can't do that!' His voice was thick with anger.

'Oh?' bridled Grace Tate. 'And why not, may I ask?'

'Because yo're goin' to marry me, that's why!' Dave snapped, and then, realising what he had said, muttered half defiantly, his face burning, 'That is ... if yu'll have me. When all this is ... over.'

Grace Tate looked at him, her eyes shining. He took her by the shoulders, and for a moment the pair of them were oblivious to the other occupants of the room.

'Miss Grace, I had no right to say that,' Dave said, 'but I do have a right to say what I'm goin' to say now. I'm ridin' for South Bend. No matter what happens, no matter what Barclay offers yu, promise me yu'll do nothing, until I get back with Judge Pringle. Will yu promise me that much?'

Grace nodded, raptly, and in the next moment, suddenly realised that she and Dave were anything but alone. Dave realised it simultaneously, and without another word, stumbled out of the house. In a moment, they heard the sound of his horse's hoofs receding down the river trail. To cover her confusion, Grace turned to the crew and told them, 'I am going to do what he said.'

'That figgers, ma'am,' said Gimpy. Whereupon Grace flushed an even deeper scarlet and fled from the room.

The towering face of the mesa frowned down on the parched desert floor below. Moving along the foot of the cliff, Sudden found himself in a long, narrow canyon which grew narrower towards its far end about a mile distant, and which looked, from Sudden's viewpoint, like a complete dead end. Above him, tumbled rocks took the form of a lizard.

'Wonder if they keep a lookout posted?' Sudden mused. 'More'n likely. Better take no chances, although I shore don't feel much like walkin' in this heat.'

He dismounted where there was shade and the horse could not be seen by any passing rider, took off his boots and began the slow approach towards the end of the canyon. By the time he reached the box wall an hour later, his feet were blistered and cut, but he disregarded these minor irritations as his keen eyes scanned the tumbled rock formations towering around him.

'Now, if I wanted to keep my eye on this canyon, I reckon I'd find me a spot with some shadow,' he mused. 'Which means on that slope over there.' Slowly, methodically, he let his eyes range foot by foot across the tumbled terrain. Lizards scuttled across the rocks as he lay motionless. A half hour went by; an hour. After another fifteen minutes, Sudden's patient scrutiny of the terrain was rewarded. About fifty yards higher up on the canyon wall, a shifting gleam of sunlight on metal revealed human presence.

'On yore own are yu?' wondered Sudden, aloud. 'Well, we better go look; I don't guess they're expectin' trouble, though.'

Inch by inch, foot by careful foot, placing his weight carefully to avoid dislodging a stone or starting a small slide which would reveal his presence, the Slash 8 man moved in a large circle around and above his unsuspecting quarry. Presently, flattened against a high round pillar of rock, the hunter was rewarded by the sound of metal scraping against stone, a man coughing. Moving carefully Sudden closed in on the guard. Prone on his stomach, he peered around the edge of the rock, and was rewarded by the sight of a burly back hunched behind a natural parapet of rock which commanded a view of the entire canyon opening. One glance was sufficient to tell the Slash 8 man that the guard was asleep. Moving like a shadow, Green closed in on the man and crashed the barrel of his gun down upon the drooping head. The guard keeled forward like a pole-axed steer, and a muffled snore emerged from his slack mouth. Sudden grinned.

'Seemed like a shame to wake yu up,' he murmured, Quickly and efficiently he bound the man's hands and feet, then began his descent towards the hidden aperture to the valley beyond which, from this vantage point, it could be plainly seen.

Back on the canyon floor, however, the screening brush effectively hid any trace of the narrow fissure in the rock walls which opened up into the hideout. Sudden shook his head in admiration.

'Shore is a dandy spot,' he told himself. 'A man could ride out here five times a week an' still not spot it.'

Thunder was waiting patiently where his master had tethered him; he greeted Sudden's arrival with a quiet nicker and tossed his head impatiently when Green mounted.

'Hopin' for action, are yu?' grinned Sudden. 'Well, where we're goin', you're shore likely to get some. Git along, yu ol' crowbait.'

The faint, almost indistinguishable trail led among tall thorn trees and beneath the gloomy face of the rock cliff. Nothing moved in the canyon except the horse and the rider; here and there a slow seepage of water had marked the red rocks, but no birds sang in this dark place. Ahead, however, was a bright shaft of sunlight, and in a few moments, Sudden rode into a wide clearing. He looked about him with interest. The valley was perhaps a mile and a half long, and almost directly through its centre ran a clear, burbling stream of mountain water. All around were sleek, well-fed cattle.

'She shore is a natural corral,' Sudden thought. 'An' I'm bettin' that these dogies ain't as near home as they oughta be.'

Turning the horse, he cantered over to one of the nearest bunches. A quick glance showed him that the brands were all new; all of them were unknown to him: Box 48, Diamond 8 were two he saw. Moving quickly in among the herd, he smoothly cut out a two-year-old and examined its brand more closely.

'Botched the job,' he told himself. 'Runnin' iron, for shore. I wonder whose brands these are?'

It was obvious whose they had been; the Diamond 8 was a continuation of the Slash 8 brand. A few deft strokes, a new brand. Box 48 could be easily made from Box B. Who owned these brands?

A frown creasing his forehead, Sudden remounted, and rode slightly to the north. Ahead, perhaps fifty yards away, stood a small cabin. Smoke spiralling from its tin chimney attested to the fact that the house was occupied, and Sudden settled down behind a clump of bushes to wait for darkness. An hour went by; then two. Three men came out of the house; one of them went to a small corral behind the house, and a fourth came out and stood on the porch. The man who had gone into the corral came out leading a saddled horse; and all four stood talking together for a moment. Sudden half-rose; it looked as if one of the outlaws was about to ride out, perhaps to relieve the guard whom he had stunned. He edged backwards, around the rock face, his eyes still upon the house and the men outside it. A jarring voice stopped him in his tracks.

'Come a-visitin', have yu?'

FOURTEEN

The urgency of his mission had lent wings to Dave's feet; he reached South Bend that same night, and found the old Judge busy writing in his study. Breathlessly, Dave told his story; of Grace's visit to the bank, the unexpected reversal of de Witt's friendship, the call-in of the mortgage; of the ambush attempt by Parr and what Parr had confessed, and all the rest. Judge Pringle listened without expression until the Slash 8 cowboy had finished.

'You say that de Witt has asked for an extra three thousand dollars on the mortgage?'

'That's right,' Dave nodded. 'Grace – uh, Miss Tate was shore that fifteen hundred dollars was the correct amount, but de Witt trotted out the papers and there it was in her daddy's fist, an IOU for four thousand five hundred.'

'And de Witt has kept this paper at the bank?'

Dave nodded again. 'I can't believe the Old Man woulda borrowed that kinda coin, Judge,' he blurted. 'He shore never spent nothin' like that much on improvements at the ranch.'

'I'm sure of that,' growled the older man. 'What you've told me tied in with some other things I've discovered. 'Now, when did you say the deadline is?'

'Brady said he'd hold the auction in Hanging Rock day after tomorrow, midday,' Dave informed the lawyer.

'I see. Then you will forgive me if I suggest that we do not need to ride overnight to the Slash 8? I am not as young as I was, Mr Haynes, and you'll forgive me if I say that you look as if you need some rest yourself. I learned some years ago that the haste we make is often lost when we get where we are going.' The old man tempered his word with a smile, and Dave nodded glumly.

'I guess yo're right, Judge, although I had kind of figgered —'

'I know, my boy. I haven't quite forgotten what it's like to be young. But rest assured, nothing is going to happen tonight at the Slash 8 if you stay here. Perhaps I should get my housekeeper to look at that bandage on your arm and then make you up a bed. We can start at first light tomorrow.'

Dave nodded again.

'And don't be downcast,' the Judge rallied him. 'I think I can promise you that we shall be able to put a halt to Mr de Witt's plans. Now ... how about a nice hot cup of cocoa?'

Dave did his best to hide his feelings from the kindly old man.

Even while Dave was on his way to South Bend, the Slash 8 had another visitor. Watching the latest arrival, Dobbs remarked to Shorty that the ranch was getting to be a regular meeting place.

'Shore, an' we get all the best people comin' to call,' replied that worthy, waspishly. 'His Majesty King Barclay. Yu reckon we oughta curtsey?'

Gimpy broke up their chatter with a promise that the first such inviting target either of them presented would be the recipient of his well-aimed boot, and walked out into the open yard to meet Barclay. The big rancher nodded to him curtly.

'Miss Tate here?' His eyes roamed across the front of the house as if he were assessing its value.

'That'd depend,' grated Gimpy, 'on who's askin'. In yore case, I ain't shore whether she is or not, but .. I'll ask.'

Leaving the burly Box B man to swallow the insult as best he could, Gimpy went into the house. He returned a few moments later with Grace at his side, and called, ' 'light down, Barclay. The boss-lady sez she'll see yu, although I'd've thought she'd be a mite more partickler.'

Barclay's rage finally broke through his surface control, and he hissed, 'Yu'd better mind yore manners, damn yu. When I'm—' Here, he stopped abruptly, as though suddenly aware that he had overstepped himself.

'Go on, Mr Barclay,' Grace said sweetly – too sweetly, had the big man had but the wit to see it – 'When you're what?'

'Why, I was goin' to say ... when I'm visitin' a lady I don't expect to have to swaller insults from stove-up freeloaders,' Barclay said quickly. 'Look, girl, I don't want to argue. I came up here for one reason only: to see you.' The emphasis upon the personal pronoun brought a faint flush to the girl's face.

'What for?' was her direct question.

Without replying, Barclay dismounted and tethered his horse. He had hoped that his proposal of marriage had intrigued her; that, in view of her circumstances, she might yet agree to it. He chose his words carefully as he mounted the porch steps.

'To offer yu my help,' he began. 'Listen, girl, I made no secret o' the fact that I wanted yu, the very first time I sat here an' talked to yu. I know of yore trouble: Brady is tellin' everyone in town how he's goin' to enjoy seein' that high-stepping Slash 8 crowd eat dirt. Is it right that yo're still shy three thousand dollars?'

'Yes, it is,' Grace said, 'although what—'

Barclay held up a beefy hand. 'Let me finish, girl. Here's the way I see it. I told yu once that with your ranch an' mine combined, we could make an empire out o' this valley, an' it's still true. Yu could be queen of the Sweetwater Valley. Marry me. I'll pay off yore debts, we'll join our ranches together, an' I'll treat yu like the queen yu deserve to be. What do yu say?'

It was a masterly speech, Barclay told himself, and he could see that he had impressed the girl. He was congratulating himself on his performance when Grace Tate's voice cut in on his reverie.

'Are you so sure that I cannot pay off the mortgage?' Grace asked sharply.

'Grace, girl, I'm the biggest man in this valley. I know to within five dollars what every man within fifty miles has in that bank. I'd be a mighty pore businessman if I didn't.' Barclay was growing expansive. He felt now that he was sure to win; nevertheless he constantly guarded against giving the girl any indication of how important it was to him that the Slash 8 was not sold in auction. She must surely see that whichever way the chips fell he would get the ranch (she could not know more). The fact that he did not own the Box B, or, for that matter, the fine suit he was wearing, bothered Barclay not a bit.

Grace, meanwhile, struggled to control her mounting distaste for this puffed and ugly man. She asked another question.

'Surely I would have to get my guardian's permission to marry?'

'Shucks, that don't matter,' Barclay smiled. 'We could marry in secret, an' yu could spring it on them later. That way, if Green is tryin' to ruin yu, I'd be around to protect yu.'

'I'm sorry,' Grace said. 'I must have time.' She watched

the rancher's reaction from beneath lowered lids, saw the explosive anger that reached his eyes, made the veins bulge in Barclay's forehead.

'Girl, I ain't the waitin' kind,' Barclay told her brutally. 'Tomorrow, they'll be sellin' yore ranch by auction. If yu want to avoid that, if yu want to hold on to what's yores, marry me today. Yu don't really have much choice.'

'You are right, Mr Barclay,' Grace said, rising. He looked at her in bewilderment. 'Of the two disgraces, however, I prefer the public to the private. I would rather be sold at auction myself than marry a liar and a cheat and a criminal, all of which I believe you to be. I will now thank you to leave this ranch.'

Barclay jumped to his feet, brow black as thunder, fists clenching and unclenching.

'Girl, yu just made the biggest mistake o' yore life. I was goin' to be kind to yu. Now, I'll see yu in hell afore I'd help yu. Tomorrow I'll throw yu out of here personally.'

'That's tomorrow,' cut in a dry voice. 'Today, it's the other way around. Grab him, boys!' The speaker was Gimpy, and behind him were grouped the rest of the crew, who wasted no time in grabbing Barclay's arms, and frog-marching him down the porch steps and across the yard, to where Dobbs had his horse waiting.

Gimpy drew his gun and told the boys to turn Barclay loose.

'Damn yu, I'll see yu all in hell for this!' raged Barclay.

'If I see yu in hell, damme if I don't ask for a transfer to Paradise,' grinned Gimpy, and without expression, he fired his gun under Barclay's horse's belly. The explosion sent the animal rocketing away down the trail to the river, with Barclay flailing to hang on. Gimpy stomped up to the house.

'He's gone, ma'am. Kinda faster than he intended, I reckon,' he grinned.

Grace's face was sober. 'He'll never forgive what I said to him,' she said. 'I pray that David has discovered something to help us. And what has happened to Green?'

FIFTEEN

When Sudden whirled to face the man who had caught him unaware, he found himself looking down the barrel of a Remington held in the rock steady hands of a hulking, broken-nosed brute of a man whom he recognised immediately as Bull Pardoe, the leader of the gang which had tried to hang George Tate that fateful night at the Slash 8. Pardoe evidently recognised his prisoner, too, for an evil smile of satisfaction creased his face.

'Well, well,' he sneered, 'if it ain't the two-gun hero himself. So you sneaked past Smitty! What brings yu up thisaway, hero?'

'Snake-huntin',' was the laconic reply, 'an' I reckon I've found a real nest of 'em.'

'Yo're probably goin' to wind up gettin' bit, too,' was the sharp retort. 'I' been hopin' to get the chance o' salivatin' yu, hero, an' damme if now ain't just as good a time as any....'

So saying, Pardoe's finger tightened on the trigger of the repeating rifle. Before he could add the extra ounce of pressure his prisoner, who still stood as though it were he who held the gun, remarked quietly.

'Don't yu reckon yu'd better wait until yore boss sees me?'

'He ain't—'

'Here – I know. It ain't no use lookin' dumb, I know yu ain't the ramrod o' this cosy li'l group,' interjected Sudden. 'Yu ain't got the brain.'

'Yu better shut yore yap,' growled the big man, 'afore I shut it. I got half a mind—'

'An' that's about all,' snapped Sudden. 'Ain't yu given a thought yet to how I found this place?'

Confusion pursued puzzlement across Pardoe's face, and the Slash 8 man pressed home his advantage.

'Curt Parr talked,' he told his captor. 'I've passed the word on, so it don't make no never-mind what happens to me. Yo're goin' to be up to yore navel in law mighty soon.'

'Yo're bluffin',' growled Pardoe.

'In which case, yu got nothin' to worry about,' said Sudden airily. 'Go on an' shoot.' He watched his man carefully.

Pardoe regained his composure very quickly, and, moving without warning, he swept the barrel of the rifle up and across, catching Sudden a glancing blow on the temple. Had the Slash 8 man not been ready for such a move, the blow might have been more damaging; as it was, he dropped to his knees, shaking his head and giving every appearance of being half-stunned. Anything which might make Pardoe relax his guard slightly was a good thing. Pardoe did not make the mistake of coming any closer, though. Instead, he jeered, 'Come on, hero, tell me some more. Yo're bluffin', an' I nearly swallowed it. Git on yore feet.'

Sudden got up, acting as though it was a painful struggle. In truth, his head was throbbing from the blow he had received. Pardoe gestured with the rifle. 'Shuck yore gunbelt. Drop it an' step away from it.' Sudden complied with the order and Pardoe rasped, 'Now march! Lead the way to the cabin, an' don't try no tricks or I'll beef yu shore.'

With Pardoe four paces behind, the rifle cocked and ready, Sudden had no choice but to comply with the order. As they neared the cabin the men Sudden had been watching came towards them.

'Look what I found snoopin' around,' announced Pardoe. 'Our two-gun friend from the Slash 8 – only he don't look so tough without his guns.' The others gathered around in a circle, and Sudden noted that one of them sported a purple bruise on his cheekbone and jaw.

'Hello, Ray,' he said cheerfully. 'Bump into a door?'

The man addressed allowed his face to twist into ugly rage, and he took a stop towards the Slash 8 man, fist upraised. A word from Pardoe stopped him.

'We all owe him,' Pardoe snapped. 'I got his mark on me, same as you others.' He touched the bullet burn along his earlobe. 'An' then there's Morley.'

'Oh, which one was Morley?' asked Sudden brightly. 'The one who took the slug in Thunder Ravine?'

'Morley's dead, damn yore eyes,' snarled Pardoe, 'but yo're goin' to be meetin' him shortly.'

'Don't' lose yore temper, Bull,' Sudden advised, coolly. 'Remember that Linkham will want to decide what to do with me.'

A chorus of agreement arose from the outlaws.

'Why waste a bullet on him,' hissed Ray. 'String him up. Give him a dose o' what Tate was goin' to get.'

'Good idea,' enjoined a lanky man on the right. 'Get a rope.'

The subject of these deliberations stood unmoved by the threatening atmosphere about him, not a muscle of his face betraying the churning thoughts flashing through his mind. Mentally he put names to the men in front of him. Ray he knew. The guard, Pardoe had revealed, had been Smith. The tall lanky man, with the slight Irish burr in his voice would be Callaghan. Morley was dead. That meant the short, bearded man in the centre and the fourth man, the one with the horse were Roberts and MacAlmon. Which of these was which Pardoe resolved with his next words, addressed to the man with the horse.

'Mac,' he grated. 'Give me yore rope.' Once again he prodded Sudden with the rifle barrel. 'Mebbe yu won't act so cool when yu start dancin' on air, hero!' he jeered. Prod. 'What d'yu say, hero?'

'I say that tryin' to hang an old man an' hidin' behind a gun are about all yo're fit for, Pardoe. No wonder yu didn't have the guts to face George Tate. Bushwackin's more in yore line.'

Pardoe smiled a slow, evil smile. 'Wrong again, hero!' he said. 'It don't hurt to tell yu now. Linkham beefed the old man, but he was really after yore scalp. In fact, he used this Remington. That's why I'm so shore he ain't gonna mind if we have a little fun with yu, since yu've been so charmin' as to come an' see us alone. Eh, hero'?' Once again he poked the rifle barrel into Sudden's ribs, but this time Sudden was ready. Imperceptibly he had been shifting his position, inch by inch, during Pardoe's diatribe, and now, with a fluid, lightning movement, he grabbed the rifle barrel and yanked it forward, pulling Pardoe off balance towards him. With a curse, Pardoe lurched forward, and Sudden locked an arm like iron about the outlaw's bull neck, and in the same movement whipped Pardoe's six-gun from its holster. Before any of the others had time to even move, they were covered by the unwavering bore of the .45, and they had looked into those deadly slitted eyes once before. They froze.

'That's better, gents,' said Sudden. His voice was like shifting ice in some polar sea. 'Now – suppose yu all very gently unbuckle yore gunbelts an' step away from them.'

During this speech he did not relax one ounce of the pressure of the arm locked about Pardoe's neck, but kept the wheezing outlaw bent backwards like a bow, the pig eyes bulging as the man struggled for air. The four outlaws faced Sudden, and for a moment they hesitated; then an imperious flick of the revolver in Green's hand convinced them that hesitation might prove fatal, and their hands flew to their belt buckles. It was in this moment that Pardoe acted.

Without warning, the big outlaw simply let his entire body go slack, and folded his knees. His weight slumped against Sudden and for a moment pulled Sudden slightly off balance. In the same second, Pardoe struck blindly backwards at the Slash 8 man with his elbows and roared, 'Get him, boys!'

Sudden, pulled forward into the wicked blows of Pardoe's ham-like arms, reeled to one side as the broken-nosed outlaw rolled clear of him to allow his fellows an unimpeded shot. He was immediately sent spinning by Sudden's first shot, which caught him high on the left shoulder and knocked him into a sitting position against the porch of the cabin, half-unconscious, but still able to see the unbelievable tableau before him.

Pardoe saw Ray yank his gun from its holster as the other three dived for cover, clutching their guns. He saw Sudden through a cloud of dust as the Slash 8 man hit the dirt and kept rolling, heard Ray's gun boom, saw Ray suddenly wilt as Green's second shot took the outlaw clean between the eyes; saw Callaghan plucked off his feet, while still running, by Green's third shot; saw MacAlmon stop, turn, and fire at Green, missing him. Green's fourth shot drove MacAlmon back against the rails of the corral, where he lay unmoving and Green was now out of sight behind a water trough in the yard. Pardoe cursed and tried to move, but the pain in his shattered shoulder kept him pinned where he was like a collector's butterfly. And he watched in agonised disbelief as Bob Roberts, who had skittered into the barn, came thrashing out on horseback, firing as he came, trying to pin the Slash 8 man down until he was out of range. Green remained unmoving behind the stone trough as Roberts' bullets whined off it or thunked huge sprays of water upwards. Within a few moments Roberts was clear of the yard and heading for the trail. Pardoe cursed again, feebly, watching impotently as Green vaulted nimbly over the trough, scooped up the Remington which Pardoe had dropped, and in one movement swept it to the shoulder and fired. Pardoe watched Roberts tumble from the saddle as though reluctant; there was a small puff of dust as the man's body hit the ground. The riderless horse careered on for a few yards and then stopped, ground hitched by the trailing reins.

Pardoe shrank back against the porch steps as the dust-smeared, slit-eyed Slash 8 man came across the yard and stood looking down at him in disgust.

'All right Pardoe – yore war's over!' he grated.

Pardoe tried to speak, but found that his voice was gone. He had been around most of the trail towns of the West, and he had seen some good men with a gun. What could he say to this ice-cold devil, whose six-gun wizardry had in one unbelievably fast battle left him the only man out of six still on his feet? Pardoe looked vainly for some indication that Green had been hit, and finding none, resorted finally to a weak round of cursing. His self-indulgence was interrupted rudely by a kick in the ribs that set whorls of pain-fire dancing before his eyes.

'Pardoe, yo're faced with a choice: I want some information. If yu give it to me, I'll promise yu a fair trial. If yu don't, I'll kill yu now.'

Pardoe nodded; he did not dare argue with this menacing figure.

'I want to know where Linkham is, and when he's due here again.'

'What time is it?' Pardoe asked, weakly.

'About six o'clock.'

'Link oughta be on his way here now, in that case.'

Sudden smiled, a cold smile that sent no answering warmth into Pardoe's face; he looks like a wolf thinkin' o' deer-meat, was the outlaw's unspoken thought.

'Then let's wait for him,' said Sudden cheerfully. 'Maybe he's got good news for yu.'

Without seeming effort, he bent, pulled Pardoe's good arm around his neck, and half dragged, half lifted that worthy into the house. When he got the burly outlaw inside, he threw him down on one of the rough straw mattresses in the bunks that lined the wall. Pardoe fell like a sack of potatoes.

'Out like a light,' Sudden told himself. 'He shore ain't as tough as he thinks he is.'

So saying, he tore Pardoe's shirt open, and using strips from it, bound the man's wound roughly. Having made the man comfortable, he then proceeded to bind and gag Pardoe efficiently in the bunk. Pardoe lay unconscious, a slight snore escaping his slack lips.

'Sleepin' beauty,' commented Sudden. 'One day yore prince will ride up on his charger. I'm bettin' he don't kiss yu.'

So saying, he hurried out into the yard to the gory task of removing the huddled bodies lying there. Having dragged the bodies into the barn, he returned to the cabin and settled by one of the windows. Cradling the Remington across his knees, he settled down to watch the trail.

SIXTEEN

Burley Linkham was in a foul mood. Just over three hours previously, he had been in Jasper de Witt's office, and once more that jaggedly sarcastic voice had flayed his ego.

'So, you gave Parr a pistol-whipping and let him go, Burley?' de Witt had said. 'Is that what you're telling me?'

Linkham had nodded. He realised from the banker's tone that he had made a mistake. Exactly how, he did not know; but de Witt's anger was unmistakable.

'It seems I cannot rely on you to do anything right, Burley,' the banker said silkily. 'First, you kill Tate instead of Green. Then, to compound your stupidity, you set Parr free with information which could hang you. You oaf! You lumbering, brainless dolt! Do I have to think of everything for you? Don't you know that Parr will tell what he knows to any fool who asks him a question? Do you think I have spent all these years perfecting this scheme to have it ruined by a fool who wouldn't know which way was ahead if he wasn't pointed?' De Witt jumped to his feet, waving aside Linkham's stammering excuses and denials. 'Be quiet, you fool! Let me think for a moment.'

Linkham lapsed into a surly silence, scowling malevolently at the pacing banker, who if he noticed his underling's looks, remained oblivious of their import.

'Where would Parr have gone?' the banker asked suddenly.

'I – I dunno, I – uh—' faltered Linkham. 'I just told him to start ridin' an' not to stop. The way he looked, I never figgered he'd do anything else.'

'He knows about the Hideout, of course?'

Linkham nodded dumbly.

'And he knows you and the others.' It was a statement, not a question. Without giving Linkham time to reply, even had the man wanted to, de Witt went on, 'Yu'd better find him, Burley. And do not come back here unless you can – without proof that Parr is dead I shall have no further use for you. Do you understand me?'

His baleful eyes fixed Linkham with a glare so evil that the roughneck, case-hardened to violence as he was, recoiled in alarm. Hastily mumbling that he would find Parr, Linkham lurched to his feet.

'What about – everythin' else?' he ventured.

'Everything else, as you put it, is under control, Burley. I can go ahead now with you or without you. It is a matter of supreme indifference to me one way or the other. Tomorrow Brady will auction the Slash 8, and Barclay will buy the ranch from the bank. The girl will probably return East. You will then take your men and ensure that the other employees of the Slash 8 are – taken care of. If, however, you are unable, for one reason or another, to take care of it, I am sure I shall be able to find someone to replace you.'

'Yu wouldn't,' breathed Linkham.

'I would, and I shall – unless you find Parr in twenty-four hours and bring me proof that he is dead. If you do that, our deal will be consummated. You shall have the Box B to run; we shall own the valley. So go, you have no time to waste. Afterwards, we shall settle our score.'

Linkham nodded, and settling his sweat-stained hat

more firmly upon his bullet head, left the office. De Witt leaned back in his chair, making a steeple of his fingers, and reflecting upon his last words with Linkham. Beautifully phrased, he told himself. You and I shall certainly settle our score, Burley. It will be a pleasure. He smiled.

Linkham saddled his horse and rode slowly out of town. His immediate worry was the whereabouts of Curt Parr. Where would the man have gone? It had been very early when Parr had appeared at the Barclay ranch; it had been mere luck that Zack had been in bed when Parr appeared, for Barclay knew nothing about Parr's spying activities. His lip curled when he thought of the way that Barclay patronised him, when all the time de Witt was playing the rancher for a fool. I'm de Witt's right-hand man, thought Linkham, and when the tally is made, I'll be in the saddle. De Witt had already hinted many times that as soon as the deal was finished, he would have no further use for the blustering Barclay. And Linkham knew what that meant. As it had been many times before, his mind was awed by the immensity and thoroughness of de Witt's planning. There was Zack Barclay fronting for him in the land purchases; Linkham himself, put on the Box B ostensibly to help Barclay, but in fact to keep Barclay under watch, and at the same time to provide him with a cover for Linkham's leadership of the Shadows. Barclay was fool enough to think that it was his own reputation that kept the Shadows away from the Box B. In fact, on de Witt's orders, Pardoe and the boys had been stealing Box B cattle in small quantities for many months. And if Zack ever stepped out of line, a lot of incriminating evidence would turn up: brands like the Diamond 8 and the Box 48 were registered in Barclay's name – and the cattle were in the canyon, ready to be revealed if necessary. If not, they would become part of the holding of de Witt's range company afterwards. Linkham shook his head; de Witt was fantastically thorough. That bank robbery: a stroke of genius. To rob your own back so that you could force a foreclosure on the only mortgage outstanding in the valley. That was clever all right. Perhaps too clever, for de Witt had given strict instructions about where the loot from the robbery was to be hidden. But Linkham had hidden the money somewhere else: that was his ace in the hole: that money would provide a man with a real life down in Mexico someplace.

But first of all, Parr. He pressed his horse forward into a gallop.

Burley Linkham did not find Curt Parr. Curt Parr found Linkham. He was camped off the trail, waiting for darkness before he ventured on the open trail again. He saw the horseman coming, recognised Linkham's paint pony immediately, and made a snap decision. If he told Linkham Green's real identity, added that Green had gone to the Hideout, that the Slash 8 man had divined the secret of the Shadows, Burley would have a chance to clear out before the John Laws arrived. He would be grateful. He would rescind his order to have Parr killed on sight. He might even review his decision about giving Parr a grubstake. So Curt Parr stood up and flagged with his arms and called 'Burley! Burley Linkham! I got to talk to yu! For God's sake, Burley, I got to talk to yu.'

Linkham reined in. His astonishment could no have been more complete if he had rubbed a silver dollar and made a wish, and immediately seen it granted. There was Parr, waving, yelling something incomprehensible, outlined clearly against the bright yellow of the sun. Linkham shot him down without a qualm and rode off, leaving the huddled form of the former Slash 8 rider where it had fallen.

He rode the distance to the Hideout in high good humour, still almost unable to believe his luck. Just to be sure, he took out of his pocket the ring he had wrenched from his victim's finger, and saw the initials CP engraved on it. He smiled, and jogged into the canyon mouth. His smile disappeared as he reached the middle of the canyon without being hailed.

'That damned Pardoe!' he muttered. 'How many times has he got to be told about keepin' a guard posted? Damned if I don't bust his beak again for him.' So saying he dug his spurs into the paint's flank and rocketed along the trail towards the cabin. He came around the bend fast and wide and into Sudden's view. The Slash 8 man stretched himself warily, and moved away from the window to behind the door. A quick glance at Pardoe showed that the man was still unconscious. The slowing thunder of Linkham's angry arrival ceased in the yard, and Sudden heard the heavy tread of the man's boots on the steps of the porch. The door burst open and Linkham pushed into the room. 'Pardoe! – what the hell—' was as far as he got before Sudden stepped out from behind the door and slashed the barrel of his six-gun downwards. Fast as his movement was, however, Linkham's reaction was faster. He was incredibly quick for such a big man, and Sudden's blow, intended for Linkham's head, bounced relatively harmlessly off the Box B man's shoulder. With a bearlike growl, Linkham snatched at his gun, but this time Green's aim was unerring, and a chop with the gunbarrel across Linkham's wrist broke the man's hold. Linkham's gun skittered across the bare board floor. Even as Sudden struck, however, Linkham was moving. His left arm came over in a lopping sweeping blow which caught Sudden on the side of the head and lifted him off his feet, slamming him against the wall. He slid backwards, scrabbling for balance, as Linkham came boring in for the kill.

His long arms reached for Sudden's throat, but the Slash 8 man regained his balance in the same instant and brought the .45 up to cover the oncoming Linkham.

The Box B foreman stopped, his piggy eyes gleaming. He looked from the bore of the gun up into Green's narrowed eyes, and then shrugged.

'Yu goin' to kill me, Green?' he asked.

'On'y if I got to,' Sudden replied.

'What I thought,' nodded Linkham, and without a second's hesitation, threw himself bodily at Sudden. Only a short, vicious punch from the Slash 8 man's left hand, which threw Linkham off balance, prevented him from finishing the fight then and there. He landed sprawling, then raised himself on one knee. He glared at Sudden.

'Yu better kill me, Green,' he growled. 'Elsewise I'm goin' to come after yu until I whup yu or yu shoot me. Are yu goin' to fight like a man?'

For a long moment, Sudden regarded this huge bear of a man. The contest would be uneven, for Linkham outweighed and outreached him. Nevertheless, since he did not want to kill the man, and it was obvious that Linkham would only fear a man who was his physical master, there was little choice. In a strange way, he found the man's courage admirable.

'Yo're quite a man, Link,' he said. Linkham saluted him mockingly as Sudden unbuckled his gunbelt. This he threw to one side, and it was fortunate for him that he did not make the reflex action of watching where they landed, for the moment the belt had left his hand, Linkham surged to his feet and rushed in again, his huge arms swinging. A flailing blow glanced off Sudden's cheek, while another set bells ringing in his ears. He retaliated with a flurry of hard, punishing blows to Linkham's paunchy middle, then skipped warily out of range of the huge ham fists. Balanced on the balls of his feet, Sudden awaited Linkham's next onslaught which was only seconds in coming. With a bull-like roar, Linkham dived at Sudden's legs and flung his arms wide in an attempt to sweep the lighter man off his feet by sheer weight. Sudden had seen Linkham's try coming, however, and was ready for it. He moved, just enough to the right, and clubbing his fists together, brought them smashing down on Linkham's neck as the huge body neared horizontal at Sudden's waist level. Linkham hit the floor with a resounding crash that set tin plates rattling on the crude shelves along the wall. He lay there for a moment, prone, gathering himself for the next onslaught.

'Why don't yu fight like a man,' Linkham gasped, ' 'stead o' dancin' around an' dodgin' like that.'

'Yu fight yore fight an' I'll fight mine,' panted Sudden. 'I ain't aimin' to get stomped to death.'

'Well ...' Linkham raised himself slowly, 'Yo're gonna be!' And he leaped yet again at Sudden, showering a tremendous flurry of blows at his opponent. To his surprise, this time the Slash 8 man did not move away, but traded blow for blow with him. For perhaps two terrible minutes the adversaries stood toe to toe, their blows smashing solidly into each other. Blood spattered the floor. Sudden's shirt was half torn from his body, his face a mass of bruises. One of Linkham's eyes was closed, the other badly puffed. Finally, sobbing for breath, the two fell apart. Sudden stood, head hanging slightly, pumping air into his labouring lungs, while Linkham swayed, his face purple with exertion, whistling for breath.

'Damn yu!' he muttered through broken teeth, 'I shoulda finished yu the night that old fool Tate got his.'

As this callous statement escaped Linkham's lips, a murderous hatred slid slowly into Sudden's eyes. The Box B man saw it, and despite his fuddled state, realised the enormity of his error. Now Green advanced upon him like a stalking tiger, his sinewy arms moving like steel pistons, driving blow after blow into the wilting Linkham.

The unconscious Pardoe had awakened during the brawl. Lying in the bunk, he whispered an awed, 'My Gawd!' as Sudden prowled forward, his blows landing with solid, merciless regularity. It could not last. Slowly, with what seemed to the watching Pardoe almost like a sigh of relief, Linkham toppled. Like an old, old tree, he leaned slowly sideways, teetered, then crashed to the scraped board floor, where he lay like a dead man.

As Pardoe watched, his eyes like saucers, the killing light faded from Green's eyes; the bandit saw something almost like regret cross Green's face. Slowly, the Slash 8 ramrod straightened up. Crossing the room he picked up his gunbelt and strapped it on.

'I reckon that's the whole story, now,' he said to no one in particular.

He seemed to see Pardoe for the first time; stooping, he untied the man's bands and helped him to his feet.

'Come along, Bull, an' don't give me no trouble. We got some ridin' to do. Give me a hand with Linkham.'

Chafing his wrists, Pardoe got to his feet and hastened to do the Slash 8 man's bidding. After what he had seen that day, if Green had told him to fly to Hanging Rock, Pardoe would have flapped his arms and given it a try rather than bring that cold, empty light back into Green's eyes.

SEVENTEEN

Hanging Rock was full to bursting. News of the forthcoming sale of the Slash 8 had aroused so much interest throughout the neighbouring area that practically everyone who could get to the town had done so. In addition, there was a large contingent of miners from Thunder Mesa, and Pat Newman was with them.

Down at Diego's Zachary Barclay was toasting his imminent ownership of the Slash 8 with his men; damning, the while, the girl who had foiled his chance to upset de Witt's complete control over his destiny.

The Slash 8 contingent arrived at about midday, and Grace Tate went immediately to the hotel, where Mrs Mulvaney, who by some mysterious means already knew about Grace's having thrown Barclay off the Slash 8, greeted her like a long lost daughter. Dave and the rest of the crew repaired to Dutchy's and were greeted with a yell of welcome from those of the miners who remembered them from the cattle drive over the mountains. Judge Pringle disappeared on some errand of his own. Pat Newman approached Dave, and drawing him to one side, asked, 'Is it true yu can't raise the money, son?'

Dave nodded miserably.

'I was looking for Green to tell him that I'd be glad to

take a few more head o' beef off the Slash 8 if it would help. Where is he?'

'I don't know,' Dave told the mine manager. 'I expected to see him here, an' if he don't turn up soon, I'm goin' to be askin' some people a few leadin' questions.'

Newman nodded, puffing on his pipe. 'Yu get in any trouble, yell. My boys will back any play the Slash 8 makes. I like that feller Green.'

'We all do,' interjected Gimpy, who had just limped up. 'But I ain't worried about him – he ain't the kind to get hisself salivated by the kind o' scum we got in these parts.'

'I hope yo're right.' Out of the corner of his eye, Dave saw Zachary Barclay enter the saloon. Behind him, puffed with his own importance, came Shady Brady, and a few moments later, de Witt came in. Dave kept his eye on the door until he saw Grace come in, accompanied by Mrs Mulvaney. Holding up his hand, he caught her attention, and the two women came over to his side.

'When will it start?' Grace asked him.

'Right about now, I'd guess,' he told her, motioning to where Sheriff Brady was climbing on to the bar. Someone beat on a table until the uproar died down.

'Folks, we're here today to conduct an auction,' announced Brady. 'Yu probably all know that the bank is foreclosin' its mortgage on the Slash 8, formerly the property o' George Tate, deceased. Are the owners represented here?'

'They are, sir,' Judge Pringle pushed to the front of the crowd, and with a courtly bow, ushered Grace Tate into one of the chairs which had been set up alongside a table.

'This is not a legal proceedin',' Brady continued. 'I am, therefore, placin' the conduct o' this business in the hands of Mr de Witt, the president o' the Bank o' Hangin' Rock.'

'Thank Gawd for that!' called someone as Brady clambered down from the bar, and Jasper de Witt rose from his chair facing Grace Tate and Judge Pringle and stood facing the room. Dave reflected that de Witt looked remarkably different, although there was no change in the man's actual appearance. It was something else, thought the Slash 8 man. An air of triumph, perhaps.

'Gentlemen,' began de Witt, 'and ladies.' This with a slight bow towards Grace Tate and the widow Mulvaney. 'As you all know, the bank was recently robbed and I was therefore reluctantly compelled to call in the mortgages of the Slash 8. The ranch was given ample opportunity to pay off its debt but has been unable to do so. I propose now to commence the business of auctioning the Slash 8. The first question I must ask is of Miss Tate here. Have you been able to raise the capital to pay off your debt?'

Grace shook her head wordlessly. Judge Pringle sat with his head bowed.

'Very well,' said de Witt. 'The amount outstanding is three thousand dollars. The bidding will start at that figure.'

There was a pregnant silence. A small disturbance at the edge of the crowd was observed as someone pushed through to the front. It was Barclay. He made his way to the table at which Grace Tate was sitting and bent to whisper to her.

'Yu won't reconsider?'

Grace shook her head. 'I would prefer to lose the ranch,' she said coldly. Barclay's face went dark with rage and he thrust Dave Haynes aside roughly and stood glowering for a moment before calling out, 'I'll bid three thousand dollars.'

'Mr Barclay of the Box B has bid three thousand dollars,' de Witt called. 'Do I hear more?' De Witt looked around sharply as Judge Pringle rose to his feet slowly. 'Do you wish to bid, sir?'

'No,' said Pringle shortly. 'I wish to give you the opportunity of withdrawing from this farce with dignity. I do not relish ruining you in public.'

'Withdraw?' De Witt's voice grew shrill, his eyes panicky. 'What do you mean?'

'Mr de Witt, I regret that you force me to do this. I have here' – he opened his document case and held up a sheet of paper – 'a signed and notarised copy of a mortgage deed effected between you and George Tate. It is dated two months before his death. The amount upon this document is one thousand five hundred dollars. What have you to say to that?'

This time a veritable uproar surged through the room. The nearest spectators craned forward trying to see the incriminating document, others pushing from behind. Brady pounded ineffectually upon a table with the butt of his revolver for order. After a moment, the Judge began to speak again, and the crowd's uproar stilled as they strained to hear what he said to the cringing banker.

'De Witt, you deliberately forged a document for personal gain. It takes only the stroke of a pen to change a figure one to a figure four. I suggest that you did this forgery solely to further the interests of Zachary Barclay, who, it appears, is the only person interested in acquiring the Slash 8 ranch.'

De Witt cringed back still further against the bar, his hands twitching at his lapels. 'I couldn't help it,' he whined. 'He made me do it. Barclay made me do it!' His outflung finger pinpointed the Box B man, who stood thunderstruck by this accusation hurled at him, from so completely unexpected a source.

'It was all Barclay, I tell you,' screeched De Witt. 'He threatened he'd send that gunman Linkham to torture me. He robbed the bank. He—'

Barclay growled an oath and stepped forward in front of de Witt.

'Yu lyin', sneakin' connivin', double-crosser!' he hissed. 'Yu've played me for a fool. I'll—' His hand moved towards his hip.

Like a skulking lizard, the banker's hand, a second before twitching on his lapels, darted inside his jacket, and reappeared holding a squat, deadly Derringer. The wicked little weapon boomed in the swift-fallen silence, and Zachary Barclay rocked backwards on his heels as the heavy slug tore through his heart. He fell like a log.

In a trice, several miners had rushed forward and disarmed de Witt, who made no struggle, but stood unresisting in their grasps while Sheriff Brady bent over the body of Zachary Barclay.

'Dead as a mackerel,' he announced. He rose to his feet, dusting his knees. 'Mr de Witt, yu didn't orta done that,' he said heavily. 'If Barclay was up to somethin', he shoulda been held for trial.'

'You saw what happened!' de Witt snapped. 'If I had not acted, he would have killed me where I stood. I shot in self-defence!'

A murmur of approval rumbled from the watching crowd, and Brady, never slow to bend to public opinion, relinquished his hold upon the banker and motioned the miners to do likewise. De Witt looked around. Judge Pringle was still on his feet.

'Sheriff,' he called. 'Mr de Witt said something just now about Barclay having robbed the bank, and forcing him to commit forgery. Since we cannot interrogate Barclay, I would like the opportunity of asking Mr de Witt a few questions.'

De Witt mentally cursed the old lawyer, but his mind was spinning like a dynamo. With Barclay out of the way, Linkham would do as he was told. Parr would be dead. The others were only in it for money. Nobody could contradict him if he told his story well. It might mean the loss of the Slash 8 for the present, but there was still just enough time. The girl would have to be killed now, of course, but Linkham would ... He dragged his wild thoughts back to the present, and resumed his cringing stance.

'It was all Barclay, you see,' he told them. 'He had sworn that he would own this valley, and when George Tate defied him, he decided to use any method to force Tate to sell.'

'How did you know all this?' asked Pringle, casually.

'Barclay told me,' de Witt explained, 'after he knew that I was in his power. I did not know at first, of course. I treated Barclay like the bank's best customer, which was what he was. Oh, there was talk about him; I attributed that to jealousy. As far as I could tell he was a successful man, and successful men are always envied. Even when those ranchers were murdered it seemed impossible that he could be in any way involved.'

'But something happened to change your thinking?'

'Yes, yes. It was about a week before the bank was robbed. Barclay came to the bank late one evening – I am often there late, working on figures – and I let him in. He acted very mysteriously, requested that I draw the shades, lock the doors, all of which I did. He told me I was very lucky; he was going to let me share his wealth when I made it possible for him to own Sweetwater Valley. I did not understand. He told me that he was going to rob the bank – and that I was going to help. He told me he would break George Tate or kill him, and he didn't care which. I laughed at him. I thought he was joking. I soon found out my error. He hit me. He hit me again ... and again. He had a riding whip. He beat me....' De Witt made his voice break. The utter silence in the saloon showed that he had the listeners hanging on his every world, and he laughed silently at their stupidity. 'Finally, he made me sign a paper saying that I had embezzled twenty thousand dollars of the bank's money to pay gambling debts. He told me that if I did not – co-operate – he would send the paper to my employers, and, as a touch of refined cruelty, to my aged parents. Gentlemen, I could not allow him to do that. The shock would have killed them.' He paused for effect, and a sly glance from beneath lowered lids showed him nothing but expressions of sympathy on the faces of most of the onlookers. Fools! he gloated. Sentimental, idiotic fools! 'The robbery was to force Miss Tate to raise money for the mortgage,' he went on. ''Barclay planned to steal the cattle she was driving as well, but Green, the Slash 8 foreman, prevented him from succeeding. He realised that having sold the cattle Miss Tate would be able to pay off her mortgage. It was then that he forced me to change the papers, and to give her no extra time to pay off the loan. There was no need for the loan to be called at all. Extra resources from the East had already arrived.'

A threatening mutter passed through the crowd at these evidences of the late Box B man's perfidy. De Witt looked about him. 'I had no choice, then. It was either do what he said or be ruined, bring grief and perhaps tragedy to my family. And then, no doubt, he would have killed me, too. I am not a man of violence. But I swore that he would not succeed. I am glad that I killed him. I am glad he is dead!' So vehement was this speech, and so sincere – for de Witt was certainly not acting as he spoke his last words – that one of the spectators called out, 'Good for yu, banker!' and several others murmured audible agreement.

Judge Pringle's voice cut through the chatter.

'Why didn't you tell Sheriff Brady about this? Or contact your Head Office?'

'But don't you see how cunning Barclay was?' de Witt

cried. 'He could have denied everything. I hadn't a shred of proof against him. The documents were forged in my hand. I had acted apparently independently of Barclay. Who would have believed me when he brought out that IOU for twenty thousand dollars? None of you would ever have believed me.'

This was a telling point, and de Witt felt he could almost warm his hands at the glow of approval which came from the crowd. He turned to Grace Tate. 'Miss Tate, I can't tell you how sorry I am for all that has passed, for all your unhappiness. I am glad to tell you that your ranch is free and clear of all debt. And all threat, I might add.'

Grace Tate found herself convinced against her will. She thrust out her hand, despite the detaining grip Judge Pringle laid upon her arm, and shook the banker's limp fingers. 'Let us start afresh, Mr de Witt,' she said, her pretty face glowing with happiness at the thought that the Slash 8 would now belong to her in her own right. Her shining eyes met Dave's.

It was at this moment that the Judge drew her back to her chair, and stood up himself, thundering, 'Mr de Witt. You have not yet told me anything about the outlaw gang which you claim Barclay led – the Shadows. Who are they? And where is the money which they stole from the Bank?'

De Witt looked around him at the curious, not unfriendly faces of the people ringing the room. Mentally he sneered at them, sheep that they were. They could never know. Linkham would never talk. He suddenly knew, with a heady sense of power, that he was to these poor fools as man is to the reptiles. And so he made his mistake.

'I know nothing of them whatsoever,' he told Pringle. 'Perhaps we shall never know.'

One second later, sheer, ice cold terror slid into his veins as a well-remembered voice, cold with disdain, called flatly across the room. 'Liar!'

De Witt looked frantically towards the door. And there, a cold smile on his face, stood the foreman of the Slash 8.

EIGHTEEN

The word hung in the silence and no one in the room was more affected by it than the man to whom it was addressed. He wheeled to present a pleading face to Brady, but the Sheriff had already bustled across towards Green.

'Now see here, Green,' he bumbled, 'yu can't say things like that—'

'Brady, yo're a disgrace to that star yo're wearin'.' Sudden's cold words stopped the lawman in his tracks. 'Get out o' my way. I want some words with that mealy-mouthed polecat over there!'

So saying, he thrust his way to the side of the Slash 8 contingent, who beamed a welcome for their foreman, slapping his back, glad to see him. In a few swift sentences, Dave explained what had preceded Sudden's arrival; the foreman's face tightened at the sight of Barclay's sprawled figure. He bent to have a whispered conversation with the old Judge, nodding from time to time as the old man told him the things he wanted to know. Then Sudden drew himself upright.

'So yu salivated Barclay,' he said to de Witt.

'That was in self-defence, Mr Green.' Some of the fright

had gone from the banker's face, and arrogance began to alter his stance. 'I must say I find the remark you addressed to me improper and offensive.'

'I'll lie awake tonight an' fret about it,' the Slash 8 man said, coldly. 'But for now, I'll add to what I said. Yo're a liar, Mister Banker. Yo're also a cheat, a thief, and a murderer.'

A gasp of sheer amazement escaped the crowd at this statement, and Brady bustled forward once more. 'Green, Mr de Witt just got through explainin'—'

'Don't tell me,' jeered Sudden. 'I'm likely to cry. If yu'll quit interruptin' there's a few things I'd like to ask our banker.'

'You may ask any questions you like, Mr Green,' said de Witt with considerable dignity. 'I regret to tell you, however, that I have no intention of answering you. You have neither the right nor the power to make me do so.'

'Wrong again, de Witt,' Sudden told him. 'I got both.' From a secret pocket in the lining of his gunbelt, he produced a silver badge, which he tossed carelessly on the table. Brady picked it up and in an awed voice read the words inscribed upon it. 'Deputy United States Marshal!'

'So that was his game,' muttered Dave. 'The ol' son-of-a-gun. No wonder he played his cards so close to his chest!' He glanced at Grace, who was covering her confusion as well as she could; he smiled to himself. 'She's recallin' what she thought o' Jim when he first met her,' he thought.

De Witt, however, was stricken harder by the sight of this mark of Green's power than any man in the room.

His mind was racing. How much did this devil know?

Sudden turned to Judge Pringle, who withdrew from his case a sheaf of documents. Sudden held them up for everyone to see. 'These are certified copies of registration certificates for the ownership of the Sheppard ranch, the

Carpenter ranch, Stackpole's Diamond S. All o' them in the same name. Yu want to make a guess at whose name, banker?'

De Witt essayed a look of surprise. 'Barclay's of course.' How had this confounded gunfighter found out about the registration? Not that it mattered; nothing could be proved.

Judge Pringle stood up. 'When Green asked me to go to Mesilla and look at these land certificates I thought he was crazy. He told me that the assumption of truth is not enough, and I see now that he was right. The name on the registrations was not Zachary Barclay, but that of a man named Seth Miller. Nobody of that name is known in this area.'

'Bah! It was probably some false name Barclay used to cover his own identity,' interjected de Witt. 'He was very cunning and devious about his business transactions. Surely you don't think he told *me* everything?'

'He seems to have told yu everythin' else,' said Sudden, sardonically. 'But it makes no never-mind. Barclay couldn't have registered that land without identification that he was really Seth Miller.'

'Maybe he was,' said de Witt, coolly. 'He didn't tell me.'

'An' yu've made shore we can't ask him,' came the dry comment. 'Another question. Do yu know a man called Bull Pardoe?'

'No. I've never heard the name.'

'Funny. He knows yu.'

'Lots of people know me, Green. I am well known hereabouts.'

A snigger escaped some of the audience, and de Witt grew more confident. He would best his cold-eyed inquisitor even yet.

'In which case, that would explain why Burley Linkham knows yu, too?'

'I know Linkham. He was Barclay's foreman. Barclay sent him in to me with messages – orders, sometimes.'

'He says he wasn't Barclay's foreman.'

'What do you mean?' So! Green had already questioned Linkham. Caution!

'Linkham says that bein' Barclay's foreman was a blind. He says that he was workin' for yu, and that yu promised him he'd get the Box B to run when yu owned the valley an' Barclay was dead.'

In the utter silence of the room, de Witt stood silent while his mind scurried around like a rat in a maze. Somehow this devil had made Linkham talk; but the day wasn't yet lost! It was still only Linkham's word against his own, the word of a roughneck against that of the respected town banker. While de Witt stood speechless, Sudden turned to Dave, and a quick word sent that worthy pushing through the crowd and out of the saloon.

'I really cannot understand why you persist in this tissue of invention, Green,' de Witt said smoothly. 'Now you are asking these people to take the word of a blackguard like Burley Linkham against mine. Whatever your authority, I am sure you are exceeding it!'

A murmur of sympathy arose from the watchers. Hearing it, Sudden realised that slowly the banker was winning the crowd's support, and that so far he had failed to force the banker to make a slip. He turned as Dave came back into the saloon, herding before him two shuffling, bound, sheepish-looking men. A shout arose from someone. 'Hey! That's Burley Linkham!'

'Who'd yu get the worst of, Burley?'

Linkham indeed looked like the sole survivor of a train wreck, and Pardoe, his arm in a sling, his clothes in tatters, looked scarcely more prepossessing. Dave shoved the two men forward into the cleared space by the bar.

'Yu claim yu never seen this man afore?' Sudden

gestured at Pardoe.

'Never!' De Witt's reply was categorical.

'An' yu know Burley Linkham only slightly?' Again, the banker's cool nod.

'Well, I know *yu*!' growled Linkham. 'I know yu damn well.'

'Bah!' snapped de Witt. 'The man's an obvious liar and a tough. How would I know anyone of his kind?'

'Because Burley Linkham was the leader of the Shadows,' Sudden told him, 'an' Pardoe here was his second-in-command.'

A rumble of anger spread across the room. Here, for the first time, the people of Hanging Rock could see before them two of the men who had terrorised the area all these months. Someone at the back jumped up on a chair and shouted 'Get a rope! String the sons up!'

Sheriff Brady leaped to his feet and held up a hand for silence. 'Any more talk like that an' the man that makes it goes to jail now!'

For once, the rotund Sheriff was not laughed at, and the spectators fell silent. Easily swayed at any time, their tempers were at fever pitch now that two of the hated Shadows were in their midst. It would take only a spark to ignite the powder-barrel, and Sudden, realising this, changed the course of his questioning.

'Linkham, who was yore boss? Who gave yu yore orders?'

'Why, him!' Linkham pointed at the banker. 'De Witt. I told yu that already!'

A perfect bedlam of noise followed this statement, as the crowd began to argue furiously among themselves.

'This is becoming intolerable, Green!' snapped de Witt.' 'I refuse to stand here and be blackguarded by these renegades.'

'Renegades, is it?' hissed Linkham. 'Damn yore eyes, de

Witt, yo're not goin' to let me swing alone. I'll take yu with me – I swear it!'

Sudden turned to face the spectators.

'There's one way to settle this. Linkham an' Pardoe have confessed to robbin' the bank. Linkham ambushed George Tate.' A small gasp of dismay burst from Grace Tate's lips as Sudden made this revelation. 'They acted, they say, on de Witt's orders. Barclay was just a stooge. On the other hand, the banker here says they're liars, an' Barclay was behind the whole rotten deal. But maybe we can still get at the truth. Neither Linkham nor Pardoe was in here when Judge Pringle read out the name on those registration papers he found in Mesilla. So: has either o' yu two ever heard the banker here called any other name except Jasper de Witt?'

'*Seth!*' Linkham shouted.

De Witt had taken several steps across the cleared space as this damning name spilled from Linkham's lips. With an inarticulate squeal of rage, de Witt wheeled and thrust his shoulder into the chest of the gawking Sheriff Brady, who reeled sideways into Sudden, blocking for a vital few seconds any effective action on the part of the Slash 8 man. In those seconds, de Witt had dragged Grace Tate off her chair, and the six-gun he had snatched from Brady's belt was pressed against the girl's temple.

'Not a move from any of you!' he hissed, 'or the girl dies. Ah, would you?' Dave Haynes, thinking de Witt's attention elsewhere, had sidled to one side to intercept the banker. The six-shooter boomed, and Dave reeled backward, clutching his arm, blood pumping from between his fingers.

'You all thought you were so smart,' sneered de Witt, unable to resist this final moment of glory. 'Yet none of you ever realised, none of you ever knew! Yes, I was the leader of the Shadows. I am Seth Miller. I came here with nothing – keep still, you!' He gestured with the pistol, and Gimpy MacDonald froze as the menacing bore stilled his imperceptible movements towards de Witt. 'Nothing – except one piece of knowledge. There will be a railroad through this valley, and the land will be worth millions, millions! And it would have been mine.' His darting eyes settled on Sudden. 'Except for one man. You are going to pay for your meddling interference. Die, damn you!'

The barrel of the pistol lifted, but even as the banker started to press the trigger a voice rang out behind him.

'*Seth Miller!*'

All eyes turned to the doorway, in which stood framed the figure of the town doctor, Patches, a shotgun at his hip. But a totally different Patches to the unshaven drunk they had formerly known. This man was sober, clean-shaven, well dressed. There was no tremor in his stance.

'Seth Miller, I've been waiting for this day for two years,' the doctor said. His tone was flat, deadly. 'Do you know me, Miller?'

The banker's face had gone ghastly.

'De Witt!' he gasped.

'Yes, Miller, Jonathan de Witt, the man whose son you murdered to usurp his name, his position, and his reputation. Are you ready to meet your Maker, Seth Miller?'

'No – don't! I'll kill the girl!' screeched Miller.

'And then I shall kill you,' said the doctor inexorably.

'No . . . no, look – I surrender. I'm dropping the gun. Look—' He thrust the half swooning Grace Tate to one side, at the same time dropping the six-gun to the sawdusted floor.

Grace Tate was quickly pulled out of danger by the Slash 8 crew as the doctor regarded the snivelling banker in disgust.

'You're not even worth killing,' he snapped, lowering the shotgun. And in that moment, de Witt's hand flashed once more to his breast, reappearing with the twin of the Derringer that had only a short while before been wrested from his murderous hand. Ere he could even level the wicked little gun, however, a shot rang out, and he faltered, half-turning to face the direction whence it had come. There, smoke wreathing from the six-shooter in his hand, stood Sudden, his eyes grim.

Painfully, with a mad hatred in his face, the dying Miller tried to raise the gun, tried to bring it to bear on the hated form of his nemesis. He had half-raised it when Jonathan de Witt turned loose with the shotgun. The blast of the shot hurled Miller in a huddled heap against the wall of the saloon.

'No offence meant, Jim,' said the doctor, 'but I figured that it was my right.'

Slowly the crowd rose from behind the tables and chairs they had dived beneath for cover when the banker had made his last insane attempt to strike at his foes.

Linkham looked down at the huddled form and turned to Green.

'Green, I don't know as I've ever seen anyone pull a gun as fast as you did in my life. He might just as well have shot hisself.'

And that was Seth Miller's epitaph.

Some days later a small gathering of the Slash 8 crew took place in the large, sunny bedroom of the ranch house. Green had come to say his goodbyes to his friend Dave, who was being nursed by Grace; Miller's shot had been only a flesh wound, but the jagged shoulder wound that Curt Parr had given the young cowboy had, so Grace Tate insisted, needed rest and attention. The knowing looks Cookie and Gimpy gave Sudden as they told him this brought deep blushes to the face of that young woman and considerable discomfort to the invalid.

'Shucks, Jim,' expostulated that worthy, 'yu don't need to go so soon. In fact, yu don't need to leave at all.'

'Yes, Jim, why don't you stay on?' Grace Tate asked. 'We'd – I'd be glad to have you here.'

'No, I ain't needed here no more. This is goin' to be a rich valley in a couple o' years, an' now that de Witt – I still can't help callin' him that – now that Miller's hold on the valley is broken, I ain't needed here.'

'How did yu ever get on to Miller, Jim?' asked Dobbs.

'Somethin' he said one time about the Shadows havin' raided the Slash 8. I knew he couldn't have found out about it from anyone here.'

'Shore was funny about Patches, though,' mused Gimpy.

'Yeah, he musta gone through hell,' agreed Shorty.

After the death of the villainous Miller, Patches had told them his story. His son, Jasper de Witt, had been sent from the East to take over a new branch of his bank in Hanging Rock. Somehow Miller, who had been hanging around in Santa Fé, making a living by gambling and as an actor, had met the young man, who had confided in him. Miller had then murdered de Witt, stolen his papers and identification, and came to Hanging Rock where he had assumed the dead man's place. Through the Bank, he had learned of the plans to build a railroad through the valley, and so made his plans.

'Jonathan de Witt – that's the feller we knowed as Patches,' explained Sudden, 'came West to find out what had happened to his son when he didn't hear from him. He discovered that the man at the bank was not his son, backtracked to Santa Fé, found out that his son had been seen around with a man named Miller, whose description was that of the man now posing as Jasper de Witt.

'But then he went to pieces. Shock, grief, perhaps fear, worked up on him. He started drinking; he was robbed.

He could not return East for help, knowing that he had no proof against Miller. So he started to play his part as the town drunk, waiting and watching for the one slip that Miller might make which would enable him to take his revenge.'

'So when Judge Pringle revealed Miller's name on those registration certificates, Patches knew Miller's time had come,' Dave put in. 'I had seen him in the saloon. He must've dodged out to get a gun. When he walked through that door, Miller musta thought he was seein' a ghost.'

'Him and his son looked very much alike,' Sudden said. 'That's why Patches was allus so dirty an' unshaven; he couldn't risk Miller recognisin' him.'

'I shore never expected Miller to have *two* shoulder guns, though,' breathed Shorty, reliving the suspenseful moments in Burkhart's saloon. 'By the way, Jim, where'd yu ever learn to use a gun like that?'

Sudden shook his head and said nothing.

'I reckon,' continued Shorty enthusiastically, 'yu could give that Sudden feller I've heard about a run for his money.'

Grace, who had left the room for a moment, returned in time to overhear Shorty's remark.

'Shorty, really!' she exclaimed, 'there's a considerable difference between a man like Jim and that dreadful outlaw.'

Sudden's smile was merry as he rose.

'Miss Grace, the next time yu see Judge Pringle, maybe yu'd tell him just that. I reckon he'd be interested to hear it in just them words.'

Grace Tate looked at her foreman in puzzlement. 'What do you mean, Jim?'

Sudden smiled.

'It's a long story,' he told her. 'Yu save it for a rainy day.'

'Oh, fiddle!' she snapped. 'You men and your mysteries. All right, now; time to go, everyone. The patient has to have some rest, and he can't rest with all this chatter and smoking. Out, out, out! You too, Jim.'

'Just give me five more minnits, ma'am. I'll be on my way then.'

'Oh – you're not leaving so soon?' Grace looked to Dave for support, and the young cowboy added his pleas to hers. Green shook his head.

'I got to move on,' he said. 'I got a job to do.'

Finally, after giving him a resounding kiss that brought a mock protest from the bedridden Dave, Grace bustled out, shaking an admonitory finger around the door. 'Five minutes, mind you. Not a second more.'

After she had gone, Dave turned to his friend.

'Jim, I got the feelin' there was more to that mention o' Sudden than yu let on. Yu want to tell me about it?'

Sudden surveyed him gravely for a moment, then a smile spread across his face. 'Shucks, yu wouldn't believe it if I told yu,' he grinned.

He thrust out his hand, and the two friends shook hands firmly.

'Take care o' her,' Sudden said. 'She's a fine girl.'

'I know it. Yu take care o' yourself, hear?' Dave told him, a catch in his throat.

'Been tryin' to all these years,' Sudden answered drily. 'I'll keep at it.'

He wheeled quickly, stopping at the door. 'Name the first one after me, huh?'

His friend lay in silence for a long moment; he heard Green's goodbyes, then his feet on the porch, and finally, the sound of his horse's hoofs pounding across the yard and down the trail and out of the valley forever. 'So long, Jim,' he muttered. 'I shore will.'